Shadow on the Highway

THE HIGHWAY TRILOGY
PART I

DEBORAH SWIFT

www.deborahswift.com

Author's Note: This is a work of fiction. Names, characters, places, and incidents are a product of the author's imagination. Locales and public names are sometimes used for atmospheric purposes. Any resemblance to actual people, living or dead, or to businesses, companies, events, institutions, or locales is completely coincidental.

Book Layout ©2013 BookDesignTemplates.com

Shadow on the Highway/ Deborah Swift.1st ed.
ISBN-13:978-1500549831
ISBN-10:1500549835

ALSO BY DEBORAH SWIFT

ADULT FICTION

The Lady's Slipper
The Gilded Lily
A Divided Inheritance

And still of a winter's night, they say, when the wind is in the trees,
When the moon is a ghostly galleon tossed upon cloudy seas,
When the road is a ribbon of moonlight over the purple moor,
A highwayman comes riding—
Riding—riding—
A highwayman comes riding, up to the old inn-door.

Alfred Noyes – The Highwayman

CHAPTER ONE

Markyate Manor

May 1651

I knew why they sent me instead of Elizabeth to Markyate Manor, though they thought I hadn't understood.

When Ralph asked Mother, I saw her lips say, 'They can't afford Elizabeth.'

If they whisper their mouths make the shapes even more clearly than when they just talk. And I'm deaf, not stupid. I listen with my eyes, that's all.

On the day I was to go, Mother walked me the six miles over to the Manor, to make sure I got there. When she caught me dawdling she grabbed my hand in her dry calloused one to tow me along. Our feet left dark footprints in the dew as we went and my cloth bag thumped against my legs as Mother's breath puffed out a rhythm of white in the chill, early-morning air.

We crossed the rutted highway to Wheathamstead, checking first for bands of soldiers. Cromwell's unruly troops often used this route and they'd trodden it into mulch. On Nomansland Common a cow rubbed its bony backside on the empty stocks and the starlings flew up away from us from the hedge with a smatter of wings. As the sun rose higher Mother speeded her step, leaning into the journey as if she could not be there quick enough. I just clutched the stitch in my stomach.

Markyate Manor slowly solidified out of the morning mist, growing grander with every step, until it swelled over us with its towering red-brick chimneys. My breath caught in my throat. It was enormous. I'd get lost in there. Mother gave my arm another tug and pulled me out of sight of the front door, her head bent, skirting the corner of the house. I tilted my neck back, trying to see the top of the domed turrets but Mother frowned at me, 'Quick! We'll be late.'

Past glazed windows which seemed to hold no reflections, past ivy hanging away from the walls. Where was everybody? There was not a soul to be seen. At the peeling back door Mother jerked on a green metal handle, I imagined a distant bell.

We waited. I wiped my face with my sleeve; I was hot from all the hurrying and it wouldn't do to look unpresentable. The door opened and Mother pushed me on ahead. In the gloom my foot stubbed on a trunk and I had to reach out a hand to the wall to steady myself. The agitated young woman who had let us in had her gloves on already, the drawstring of her cloak was tied up tight around her neck, and all her bags stood in the hall.

'I'm Mrs. Chaplin and this is Abigail,' Mother said.

'Henshaw, that used to be the maid,' the woman said, and sniffed, as if I smelt bad. 'The wagon will be here any moment, so I won't wait.' Her words were clipped, as if she was biting them off, so I had no trouble reading them.

I knew from the maid's expression that Mother said something in reply, but Mother was behind me so by the time I whipped round, I'd missed it.

'Lady Fanshawe knows she's coming, doesn't she?' Henshaw said, squeezing past us so that we had to flatten ourselves to the wall, 'So I'll not wait to give an introduction.'

'But what about the other staff, will the Lady not –' Mother stopped speaking abruptly and I was just in time to see the maid's words, 'Other staff? What other staff? There's only the cook indoors, and the grooms in the yard. No one else will stay.'

We watched Henshaw drag her trunk bumpety-bump down the step.

'The housemaid,' Mother explained to me from habit, though I had understood well enough, 'she's the housemaid that's leaving.' Mother's face wrinkled in consternation.

She tapped me briskly on the arm and set off down a long shadowy back corridor. At each open door she peered inside searching for a sign of life. She was as nervous as I was. I could tell by the way she had one hand clamped tight to the neck of her shawl as if it might take fright and fly off. Finally I smelt something cooking and put my hand on her shoulder.

'Down there,' I whispered, pointing down some servant's stairs.

Mother prodded me to go ahead of her. The stairs wound to the left and at the bottom I followed my nose and found my way into a vast kitchen. The cook spun round from where she was bending over a pot on the fire, her spoon dripping white lumps onto the flagstone floor.

'You gave me a start,' she said.

She was thin as a splinter, her apron strings tied twice round her skinny middle. She turned back to the fire and the cooking, but I could see she was talking by the way her back moved like a bellows.

Mother turned me by the shoulders to mouth at me, 'She's the cook. I'm to leave you here, she'll show you to your bedchamber.' She mimed 'sleep' with her hands pressed palms together next to her ear, as though I had become a child again.

I nodded, but my mouth trembled as I smiled at her. Now I'd come to it, I didn't want Mother to go home without me.

She kissed me hard on both cheeks as if to stamp the kiss into my skin. 'I'll send Ralph in a few days to see how you're faring. Do as you're told, and make sure you ask if you don't understand.'

Her face crumpled as she picked up her skirts to go out, but she turned away in the gesture she always used when she didn't want me to see her expression.

I wanted to shout after her, 'Don't leave me here, take me home again.' But of course I didn't. I just gave a sort of wave. The skinny cook by the fire kept on stirring, and I watched Mother's familiar sturdy back and then her frayed hem and then the iron soles of her clogs disappear up the stairs.

I stood in the kitchen next to my small holdall and looked about. You could see there were no servants because everything was filthy. A long rack hung the length of the chamber with dusty cooking pans dangling there. Strings of cobwebs swayed from the ceiling to the rack. By the fireplace squatted two ancient barrels of the sort for salted fish or meat, but they couldn't have been used for a while because everything was covered in soot fallen from the chimney.

A sudden movement alerted me to the fact that I was being talked to, or should I say, at, because the cook was obviously angry. She snatched the pot from the fire and dumped it on the hearth so that the porridge sloshed over the edge. I caught something about it being 'spoiled' before she gestured at me to bring my bag.

Up the stairs she marched, and I leapt to do as she asked, following her like a scared whippet, fascinated by her grey greasy plait that swung from under the flap of her bonnet. Up, up, up - to the top of the house, along passages dark with panelling, watched by old portraits of men in ruffs and images of the Virgin Mary with her sad weeping face.

Finally we arrived at a tiny box-room with a slit of an eye for a window. The bed was a bare wooden trestle with a straw mattress, the walls plain whitewash. Worse than at home, I thought. At least our house was clean. I set my bag down on the bed and looked around for a candle-holder, but there was none. My stomach turned a somersault. If there was one thing I hated, it was the dark.

The cook pointed to herself. 'Mistress Binch.' I bobbed a curtsey like I was supposed to. She stared as if surprised, but then decided it displeased her. 'Stop dawdling and get out your apron,' she said. Her mouth was small as a hen's bottom and it was hard to read her, but I opened up my bag and drew out one of my cover-alls and held it up with a questioning look.

She nodded, satisfied, then gestured for me to follow again, and off we marched doing the whole journey backwards with me tying my strings round my waist as we went. In the kitchen she passed me a tray with a bowl of the congealed porridge. Her thin hand slapped a hunk of bread and butter next to it and a pot of honey. Was it for me, I wondered? I was hungry. But no, Mistress Binch was gesturing at me to follow again.

She stopped outside an imposing door on a long corridor and waited for me to knock. The door had no give, it was solid under my knuckles as though I was rapping on the trunk of a tree. I had no idea if anybody answered, but Mistress Binch seemed to think they had, as she nodded at me and turned to go in response. I twisted the brass handle and pushed hard on the door with my hip. It swung open.

It was as though I had suddenly shrunk. Another lofty room. Down the centre ran a long board for dining, and I counted twelve chairs but none were occupied. The floor was strewn with dusty, crumbling herbs that caught in my hem as I walked. Uncertain, I put the tray down on the table. What should I do if there was no-one here to eat the porridge? I couldn't take it back. Mistress Binch would be angry. I leant a hand on the table to anchor me in the big space and stared round.

The room was still. I plucked up courage to cross the empty space to the window. There was an oak tree not far from the house, with a girth the size of a wagon wheel. I looked out beyond it to where our house must be, somewhere past the common, hidden by the tree and a scrub of woodland. Mother would be hurrying home. There would be no husband to welcome her. Father had been lost in a skirmish in Scotland, fighting for Parliament.

I wished I was back there now, to help Mother churn the butter, and to hear her tell my brother Ralph he was not driving the oxen right. Everyone had to work so hard since we lost our house. But I did not want to think of that, it hurt too much. I stood a while, fiddling with edge of my neckerchief, my head cocked to one side as if I might hear them, hear anyone.

Maybe I should take the porridge back. I turned, and there, sat at the table, was a young woman, watching me through narrowed curious eyes. The bowl was already empty.

'I suppose you're Chaplin,' she said, waving her spoon. Then, speaking very slowly and deliberately as if to a simpleton, 'Curtsey, if you please.'

My face grew hot. I did as she asked, but did not dip my head. I kept my eyes fixed on her mouth.

'Can you understand me?' She did not wait for my answer. 'Tell Binch the porridge was cold. Cold. And light a fire in the yellow chamber. It's in the west wing. A fire. West wing.'

'Yes miss.'

'Yes, m'lady. And speak up.'

I repeated it. My heart thumped in my chest. This surely couldn't be Lady Katherine, could it? I was expecting someone much older. This flame-haired girl was probably only sixteen or seventeen - a year or two older than I. But of course she had that manner they all have, of looking at you as if you are a long way off and not right under their noses.

When I got nearer I saw her lace cuffs needed a good wash. But I did not dare get a proper look, I slid the tray away and hurried out of the door. Just being near her made me nervous – the way she'd appeared from nowhere like a ghost.

In the kitchen the fire had dwindled to an ashy glow, and the pot stood on the hearth untouched. There was no sign of Mistress Binch. I wondered if there was time to eat that porridge. My stomach growled with hunger.

In the end I did not have the courage. There was nobody to show me what to do. Panicky in case I should be slow, and the girl displeased, I grabbed a pail from by the kitchen door and ran outside to search for the coal cellar and the wood store.

I lugged the full bucket down a maze of corridors, sensing the weight of the house, all that masonry, pressing down above my head. I had to find the west wing. I knew the sun rose in the east so it had to be on the opposite side of the house.

Luckily, I felt the draught of a door opening and caught a glimpse of a green silk skirt as the girl disappeared into one of the rooms. I followed, panting. The bucket made my arms ache.

It was a chamber for reading or study. The girl's eyes rested on me the whole time as I knelt in front of the fireplace. Then I realised. This small bucket would not be enough to fill this grate, would it?

I'd been used to our little fire at home, not to making great bonfires like this. Still, I got it lit, and it took. The girl sat a long way away from it on a cushioned chair, with a writing slope resting on her knee. I felt like telling her to stop watching me, and mind her own business, but of course I couldn't, could I?

Instead, I stood and turned to face her, ready for more instructions. Because if she was the daughter of the house, I was determined to show her I was the best maid-servant they'd ever had.

'Fetch more coal and wood, and then make a start on the laundry. The buck tub is outside somewhere...near the dairy. The linen basket's on the landing near my upper chamber.' She was still speaking very slowly, though she had no need, hers was the kind of expressive face that showed every mood. Like the sky, with clouds passing over.

I nodded to show I'd understood. 'When it's done, come back here and wait by the door in case I need you again.'

'Yes m'lady.'

She put down her writing slope and stood up to study me. 'Can you hear me? They told me you were deaf.'

'Yes m'lady, I mean no m'lady.'

Her brows furrowed in irritation. 'Well which is it? Are you deaf or not?'

'I can read lips m'lady.'

She raised her eyebrows and looked pleased. 'Good. We'll be able to talk. Mr Grice didn't want me to have another servant whilst my husband's away – he thinks it's a waste of good money. I frightened the last one away.' She laughed, as if it was a jest. 'But it's so boring with no female company. And the house needs a good clean.' I carried on watching in fascination, her rosy lips and little white teeth, unable to look away just in case she had more to say. 'Well, what are you waiting for?'

That was me dismissed. She sat back down with her paper and quill and began to write.

I plucked up courage and asked, 'Beg pardon m'lady, but are you the Lady Katherine?'

She looked up. 'Of course I'm Lady Katherine.' Her eyes flashed. 'Who else would I be?'

CHAPTER TWO

A Toss and a Tumble

It was clear enough Lady Katherine had chosen me to be her servant because I was cheap, not because of anything in my skill. Not because I was clever or because I could read and write, or because anyone had recommended me. I squashed the prickle of disappointment and threw more wood from the log pile into the bucket. And a Mr Grice, whoever he was, didn't want me here.

But I mustn't think. I must be grateful they'd employed me at all, and remember I owed it to Mother, so she had one less mouth to feed and worry over. She had her hands full enough with baby William and little Martha. The thought of Mother made me pause mid-movement, and press my hand to the bib of my apron to stop the pain.

It was my fault we had to live the way we did, and now was my chance to make up for the terrible thing I'd done. I would save up all my wages and pay it all back to her somehow, even if it was the last thing I ever did.

I took two more loads of coal and wood back to the yellow chamber. Such a lot to remember. My head reeled with it all. By the time I got there the first logs were burnt out and the room was still cold as a tomb. I could not help letting out a cry of frustration, but Lady Katherine ignored me.

When I'd lit the blasted fire again, even then she did not snuggle up next to it where it was warm. I had to bite my lip not to tell her. Still, maybe she did not want to get her fine silk gown full of smoke. Over it she wore a tawny velvet cloak lined with rabbit fur, and I suppose she must have been warm enough.

Later, as I lugged yet another cauldron of boiling water across the yard, I saw my mistress pass the stables. She was dressed in a heavier cloak and a hat tied down over her dark curls, its scarlet feather shivering in the breeze.

I paused in filling the laundry tub to watch her ride by. She rode a big-boned black horse with a white blaze. No stable boy was with her, no farm hand. But she looked confident, capable. She swayed upright in the saddle like a man; she used her whip smartly, her mouth opened in a command and the horse broke into a trot.

Her dark shape sped away across the field, her bronze hair flying from under her hat, skirts trailing to one side. The horse flew like lightning, straight towards the blur of the boundary hedge. Surely she wasn't going to jump that? I stared amazed as she did not even slow. The horse sailed over the hedge, her ladyship still pressed to the saddle. The last image that stuck with me was the flash of the horse's heels and the red plume of her hat.

I let out a long whistling breath. My astonishment was soon followed by irritation. The thoughtless madam. She'd gone out, when I had lit a fire and dragged heavy coal all the way from the outside store. The fire would be blazing away with nobody to see it. Why on earth ask me to do it, when she was going out?

I stomped inside to fetch the dirty linen, still cross at my wasted effort, but soon slowed. The house seemed to be waiting for something, holding its breath. I traced my name in the dust on the windowsill. I wondered if my mistress would be displeased I could write. I knew it was not something expected of a housemaid. Then fearing it might cast some sort of hex, and would tell the devil where I lived, I rubbed it out again with my sleeve.

While she was out I took the chance to explore, tip-toeing down the empty corridors, brushing spider-webs from my face. Cleaning this place would be an enormous task, and there was only one pair of hands – mine.

In the east wing, when I creaked open one door, a pile of weaponry and armour lay in the middle of the floor. I took in a gleaming halberd, some muskets and shot, even a scythe glinting there in light from the crack in the shutters.

That would teach me to pry, I thought.

I shut the door hurriedly. I did not want to know. Did not want to feel obliged to report what I had seen to anyone in the village. Like my family, the villagers were all fixed on fighting for Parliament and would be desperate to get their hands on these, if they only knew they were there.

Mother had told me that the Fanshawes were Royalists, for the King, so she had warned me to keep quiet about where our sympathies lay.

'Folk like us can't afford loyalties,' she said, 'not any more. Not if you want to keep your place.'

By lunchtime my good dress was drenched from cuff to shoulder. I found aches in parts I didn't know I had, as I dragged sodden linens out of the tub to run them through the mangle and spread them on the hedges next to the drive to dry. The wind whipped up and the sheets flapped against me as if they had minds of their own. I had to tie the corners to the hawthorn branches to stop them blowing away.

I had just finished and was praying that it would all be dry by nightfall, when my mistress cantered across the field towards me. She had taken off her cloak and it lay across the horses withers; her cheeks were flushed pink, her face merry.

She was just about to dismount when the wind caught under one of the sheets and it filled like sail. The horse leapt sideways, half-rearing in fright. I grabbed for the sheet but the wind was too strong and the end of it billowed out to flap right in the horse's face. It reared again, hooves thrumming the air.

Lady Katherine clung to the pommel, but no sooner had it landed than the horse bucked and threw her, bolting off towards the yard, tail stuck up like a flag.

My hand was over my mouth. Lady Katherine did not move, but lay on her back on the wet grass. Thoughts flew. Was she winded? Dead?

What would I tell them at home, that I'd caused the death of my mistress on my very first day? I backed away, not knowing what to do. Then good sense flooded back to me and I rushed forward to help.

A flurry of petticoats and she was up, startling me, brushing herself down, rubbing her back. She saw me staring and began to shout. Her face was white as whey, her green eyes boring into me. I was too terrified to take in her words, just saw her mouth open and close, her riding crop pointing at me accusingly. I moved away, my face frozen.

Finally I was able to make sense of what she was shouting. I was stupid. There were racks in the orchard, for drying. She wouldn't forgive me if Blaze was hurt. The horse, I realised, she was worried about her horse. I opened my mouth to apologize, but she did not give me time,

'Take the laundry to the orchard,' she shouted, 'out of my sight.'

In my hurry I stumbled, scratched my arms and tore my sleeve on the hedge trying to gather the dripping sheets in my arms.

Lady Katherine watched a moment, lips pressed together, turned on her heel and marched off towards the stables. I could see patches of wet staining the back of her green silk dress.

My legs were so shaky I could hardly walk. When I got to the orchard I could see the drying racks hung from the trees, calm and orderly. I should have thought - that in a house like this they wouldn't just spread the linen over bushes like we did at home. I was stupid, like she said. I'd only been here a morning and already I'd got it wrong. And worse - my new mistress could have died. What if she'd broken a bone?

A hollow feeling sat in my stomach. I hadn't tended the fire in the study either; Lady Katherine was cold and wet and the fire would be out. I sagged, wondered how long it would be before she sent me home.

After I'd finished hanging out the laundry I was too scared to go up to Lady Katherine. I went to check on her horse though, to make sure no harm had come to it. Blaze was a fine dark bay with a white face.

'Sorry,' I said, reaching towards his muzzle.

He side-stepped and rolled his eyes.

I stood silently and waited with my arm outstretched.

After a moment he shook himself and offered his head to be stroked. I was good with horses, always had been. My brother Ralph let me ride his horse sometimes and I loved that feeling of sitting on top of the world. No harm seemed to have come to Blaze so my heart stopped its hammering a little. He snuffled up the grass I tore for him from the verge and blew at me through his nose with his hot breath. I rubbed his ears and he nuzzled me back.

When I thought Blaze and I had made friends, I went back to the kitchen, with a vague hope that the porridge might still be on the hearth. I was ravenous. There was the smell of baking and Mistress Binch was there, hands on hips, scowling, as if she'd been waiting especially for me to arrive.

'Where's my pail?'

'Beg pardon, Mistress. I took it. To get some coal.'

'I've been looking for it all over, to mop the floor. And shut that door. Do you think we live in a barn? Go and fetch my pail. Have you never heard of a coal bucket? Don't be touching my things, do you hear? That's not a – '

Her mouth snapped open and closed like a trap, but I didn't want to know any more. I'd have to brave her ladyship and fetch the pail from upstairs. I tried to creep in to the study without Lady Katherine seeing, but she pounced on me as soon as I put my nose through the door.

'The fire's out. And I asked you to wait at this door. Where've you been?'

'Hanging the laundry, m'lady.'

'All this time? You'll have to be quicker than that. Tell cook I'm ready for my meal. Bring it to the dining room.' Impatience made her forget to speak slowly.

I cringed away, and made a hurried bob. Down all the stairs back to the kitchen where Mistress Binch clucked her lips and frowned at the fact her good pail was full of coal dust.

'Please mistress,' I asked, desperately, 'Where's the coal bucket kept?'

She answered me but with her head turned to the bread oven.

I asked again, and she turned and spat at me, 'In the main chamber, like I said.'

I served Lady Katherine her meal of pie and pease pudding with my own stomach churning and empty. Mistress Binch did not offer me anything to eat and there seemed to be no time to stop anyway. As soon as I had cleared the dishes I was to clean the pewter and then beat the rugs. The fires were always smoking and on the verge of going out. Lady Katherine kept moving from room to room and demanding fires be lit in each one.

As twilight came I was still on the run up and down the corridors and the coal bucket was never out of my hand. Lady Katherine summoned me from where I was bent over the hearth by stamping hard on the ground. I felt the tremor of the floorboards and turned in time to see her do it again. It got my attention, but it made me angry inside. Seeing her stamp like that reminded me of a small child who could not get her way.

'Chaplin,' she said, pacing up and down the room in front of me, and speaking very clearly, 'A message came. My husband will be home the day after tomorrow, with my step-father and their servants. Wednesday. The day after tomorrow. You will have the house clean and ready. You're to help Mistress Binch and you will serve us at table. I take it you know how to do that?' She did not wait for an answer. 'And fetch me hot water. My back hurts like the bloody devil.'

She turned and watched me from the corner of her eyes to see my reaction to her oath.

I coloured, remembering. The words were out of my mouth before I could stop them. 'Yes m'lady, sorry m'lady. It was the wind. It just snatched the sheets right out of my hand. I didn't mean to frighten your horse.'

A moment passed between us, a moment where she was just a girl looking at me, a girl who might smile and forgive me. But she tossed her head, quashed it. Her chin rose as she said, 'Bring the water. And you'd better turn back the bed and light the rush-lights.'

I was back in my place in an instant. 'Where, m'lady? Where would you like to wash?'

'My chamber of course.'

I didn't want to light another fire that day. 'It might be warmer in here.'

She glared. 'What a foolish idea. I'm not undressing in the study! Certainly not. Light the fire in my chamber.'

So when I wasn't carrying coal I was carrying water. As night fell the house became a labyrinth of black shadows. Pools of grey moonlight crept in through the windows. I kept glancing over my shoulder to check there was nobody there, fearful of what else might lurk in all those dark corners. Everyone in the village knew that Markyate Manor stood on the site of an old monastery, but I tried not to think of the spectre of the murdered monk. Folk said he glided through the solid walls as if they were not there.

Lady Katherine's chamber was not a very cheerful place. Grand yes, the ceilings had icings of ornate plaster, but the walls were damp and peeling. What had happened? Why was everything so run-down?

Lady Katherine arrived after I had lit the fire and the rushlights, and just as I was smoothing out the bed. I was proud of the way I had the jug of hot water already standing by.

'Unlace me.' She stood in front of me and turned, obviously expecting me to undress her, but my mouth was dry at such a prospect. I did not dare to touch her with my rough, chapped hands. Her hair fell in soft coppery tendrils over the eyelets of her bodice.

I unlaced her as she fidgeted. I helped her out of the bodice and the skirt, noticing how she shivered with the cold. She pointed at the basin and I fetched it over with the linen cloth, but I stood there, not knowing how to wash her. Which parts should I wash?

She turned and snatched the cloth from my hand. 'Oh, for heaven's sake.' She rubbed vigorously at her neck and her face, then her arms. As she scrubbed, the back of her chemise gaped open and I saw faint criss-crosses of white scars. That was shocking enough, but down below there was a big purpleish bruise across her back. I gasped. I had done that. To Lady Katherine Fanshawe. I was horrified.

She swung round. 'What's the matter?'

'Nothing m'lady.'

'Then fetch me a towel and clean linen. If I stand here uncovered who knows what disease may find its way in?'

I wiped gently, and saw her wince. She turned and pulled the cloth from my hand. 'Not like that. You're too clumsy.'

'There's a bruise m'lady.'

'It's nothing. I've suffered worse.'

I lowered my eyes and she threw the cloth back in the basin. She confused me, this child-woman with the arrogant look. And she was never still, full of a strange restlessness. There was a trunk in an adjoining dressing room and I rummaged inside, glad to find a dry cloth and a clean nightdress.

I held out the cloth for her to dry herself but she shook her head. Her foot tapped on the floor and her eyes showed she was thinking of something else. 'When my husband Thomas is home, you will sleep here,' she announced.

She seemed very young to be married, but I curtseyed to this order and bunched up the nightdress for her to put her arms through the sleeves. 'You can bring your bedding down,' she said. 'And you are to help me move that chest against the door.' Her hands fluttered as she talked.

There was another door in the wall opposite the dressing room, and she saw me look to it.

'Yes, that's his room. My step-father has the key.'

Her face showed she did not like him. I tied the strings at the front of her gown in a bow.

'Both doors,' she said, looking into my eyes. 'We'll secure both doors.'

When I left Lady Katherine it was full dark. Coming out of her well-lit room was a shock and I took a moment to steady my breath. I gripped tight to the banisters with one hand, the basin of dirty water slopping in the other, reaching out for the steps with my toes.

There was not enough light to do chores, though Mistress Binch had left unfinished pewter on the kitchen table with the sand and sawdust for polishing. A stub of candle was in one of the drawers so I lit it gratefully, and sat on a kitchen stool a moment, feeling the pressure lift from my feet. I was bone-weary. The remains of a meal lay on the table, and I crammed an edge of pie-crust and some cold pease pudding into my mouth with my fingers.

The doors in the house were well-bolted by Mistress Binch, except the back door, so I slid the bolts home. Shielding my precious candle, I wound my way upstairs. The door opposite mine was closed. I guessed Mistress Binch lodged there.

My room was as I'd left it, flickering now in the light from my single flame. It seemed like twelve months since I'd first set foot here, not only twelve hours.

I did not undress, but took my cloak from its peg on the door. I flung myself onto the bed, but there was no softness or bounce, just the planks. The thin straw mattress smelled of mould, so I spread out my cloak on it and lay down, watching the candle-flame dance. I prayed that if I closed my eyes to sleep the candle would not set anything alight. At night I was always caught between these two fears – the fear of fire and the fear of waking in the dark.

Nobody except a deaf person knows how it feels to lie in the inky blackness, unable to know what has woken you, unable to hear, unable to see. The way the dark closes in as if you're locked in a box, muffled from the rest of the world, and the fear that some danger might be behind you, and you'd never know until it was too late.

I thought of home; Mother and Elizabeth sleeping companionably, their shawls tangled together, and of my brother Ralph, downstairs on the proddy rug, his long legs spread out before the fire, feet still in his boots, his sword ready in case of trouble. I missed them already with a hollow pain below my ribs that made me clutch my side to keep from crying. Outside, an owl flashed by my window. I felt the fear in my chest fluttering hard to get out.

I wound my fingers into the cloak, holding it tight as if it might shield me against the night terrors. Thomas Fanshawe was coming with his stepfather and there was all that huge house to clean before they did. How could I do it all with no help? I heard Ralph's voice saying , 'you can do it, Abi', the way he used to when I was struggling with my letters, or learning to form new words with my lips.

I pictured my brother's smiling face, his tousled hair - my wayward brother who was always caught in the grip of some new-fangled idea or other, and never listened to a word anyone said, except to me. He always made time to listen to me. Perhaps because of what happened to me, and because I didn't talk much. He talked to me when he needed to discover something for himself – he'd lay it out before me like laying out a fleece for inspection, thinking I could not really hear, and I'd read his lips even more easily when he spoke slow and soft.

And it was Ralph who'd encouraged me to read Mother's recipe books, though it was hard, so I wouldn't lose my language. He wanted me to learn the look of folks' words on a page. The dancing letters that matched the shape of people's lips.

I steeled myself, set myself to pray. I prayed for forgiveness as I did every night. God had already punished me by bringing me the spotted fever. Four days I had fought the demons of the disease, but when I had awoken, the music had left my life. No more creak of the sails on the windmill, no more lowing of cattle or the ripple of my brother's laughter. No more birdsong. So I had to pray, with all my heart. Perhaps then God would forgive me and my hearing would return.

I pinched the candle out with my eyes closed, so I could pretend I liked it here at the manor, that I'd chosen the dark myself and it was still daylight beyond my eyelids. Then I put my face towards the window determined to waken at the first inkling of light.

CHAPTER THREE

Diggers' Dreams

I was awake long before dawn to wash myself at the well and because I was too scared of the day ahead to go back to sleep.

Mistress Binch had left porridge bubbling, but was out of the kitchen. I took the pot off the heat whilst I scrubbed the pewter from the night before and milked the five cows. There was too much milk for such a small household, but I put some in the butter churn and some to sour before serving the porridge.

Mistress Binch arrived back with some eggs, complaining before she had even shut the door. 'Look at the place,' Mistress Binch said to me. 'There's grass growing in the gutters, the vegetable garden hasn't been sown, and Mr Grice won't let Lady Katherine take on more servants. And when I asked her yesterday how I was to manage to feed Sir Simon and all his serving men with no help in the vegetable plot, she just shrugged and said, I don't know. Ask Mr Grice.'

'Who is Mr Grice?' I asked. He was the man who didn't want me here and I was curious to know more about him.

'He's the overseer that looks after the house and looks to Lady Katherine whilst her menfolk are away fighting. He's been with the family for years. Here – get these boiling in the pan.' She thrust the eggs at me. 'He was her guardian too when she was smaller, so there'll be no riding out like a wild thing when he's back, I can tell you. She'll have to behave like a proper lady then.'

'Is he fighting with her husband for the King?' I'd broken one of the eggs and it was swirling round in the water. I tried to fish it out with a slotted spoon without Mistress Binch seeing.

'No. Mr Grice was wounded at the battle of Naseby, so he can't fight.'

I struggled to make out the rest of her words, because she kept turning her head whilst she was putting things away. 'Mind, he slashed down a whole band of round-heads .... cut him off his horse. Praise God, he got away, but lost his foot. Terrible thing. He's sharp as a falcon, mind, despite all that.'

I managed to get rid of the broken egg into the pig bucket. She turned round and I put on my innocent face.

'These days nothing comes from Grice's purse without Sir Simon's say so,' she said. 'Not unless it's for weapons for the young King.'

'When will Mr Grice be back?' I said.

Already I did not like the sound of him.

'I don't know. But you'll know when he gets here, because the whole house sits up to take notice. Now, stop standing about and...' She turned away to the sink and then gave me a mouthful of instructions that I didn't catch.

'Beg pardon, Mistress?'

She turned again and spat out more words. I caught, 'silver,' 'polish', and 'board'. But I still did not really understand. I twisted my apron in my hands and begged her, 'Please, would you say it more slowly.'

This made Mistress Binch even crosser and her words shot out twice as fast. Too embarrassed to ask again, I hurried from her sight and through to the main chamber. I was relieved to see three rows of ornate silver spoons laid out there on the table. It was a fine collection, such as people show guests to prove their wealth in company. We'd had some like it ourselves, before the accident...

I pushed that thought away. I must hurry with this if I was to sweep the house too. Next to the spoons was a small glazed pot with a lid. I searched for a polishing cloth and saw one on the sideboard. This must be what she meant. I'd to polish the spoons.

I lifted the lid of the pot and saw it was filled with a greasy brown paste. It smelt foul. I sat on the bench and scooped the spoons into my apron. They had a family crest of horseshoes and a motto I recognised, 'Dieu

Donne' which I knew meant 'God Gives,' implying of course that God also takes away, something I knew only too well.

I dipped my cloth in the pot and slathered a generous quantity of the paste over the first spoon.

I was just putting polish on the last one when the light from the doorway disappeared and it made me glance round. It was Mistress Binch, an expression of outrage on her face. Instinctively I stood up.

'What are you doing?' she said.

'Polishing the spoons... like you said.'

She was over at the table in an instant. 'I said to put them away! In the cupboard! What's this?' She picked up a spoon and it slipped from her fingers. 'What the...?' My face fired up with heat as she pounced on the pot of polish. She thrust it under my nose, her eyes popping, 'My duck liver paste! It was just setting. I'd left it there to set. And you've stuck a dirty rag in it.'

I backed away. But she followed me, jabbing her finger towards my chest, her eyes accusing. 'Do you know how many ducks died to make that? It was for tomorrow's dinner. And you've used it on the spoons –'

The realisation of what I'd done robbed me of words. I cringed back against the wall. Mistress Binch was opening her mouth wide now, so wide I could see the gaps and black stumps of teeth.

'I can't believe it. How dare they send me some witless numskull who can't even follow orders? Isn't my life hard enough?' She turned from me, unfastened her apron and threw it down on the table. 'That's it. Enough. Lady Katherine can find herself another cook.'

'No. Oh please don't do that.' Shame flooded through me. 'I didn't understand. I'm going. I should never have come. Sorry Mistress Binch, sorry.'

I fled from the room, past the stiff figure of Mistress Binch and out through the back door. I ran and ran until I was out of sight of the house and then I leant on a five-barred gate and tried to stop the hot tears seeping from my eyes.

I pressed my hands to my burning cheeks to cool them. I was never going back there. The humiliation of it, to do something so foolish. I'd have to go home. But the thought of going home scared me too; Elizabeth would laugh and poke fun at me with her sharp tongue, and what would I do then, where could I go? I'd never be taken on again, not after this. The stupidity of it. I'd never live it down.

When I pushed open our cottage door Ralph took one look at my face and said, 'What happened?'

It was such a relief to see his dear face and his easy familiar way of speaking that tears sprang to my eyes again, but I caught hold of myself in time. For Jacob Mallinson was there too, at our table, and I did not want him to see them. That would be just too shaming.

'I'm just going,' Jacob said.

'No, it's all right.' I pulled myself together. I liked Jacob, he was dark and handsome and just to look at him gave me a breathless fluttery feeling inside. I hoped I did not look like I'd been crying. I tried to be casual, behave normally. I took a deep breath and said, 'Shall I get you some small beer?'

Jacob grinned and said, 'Now that's a nice thought.'

'Where's Mother?' I asked.

'Luton, at the market,' Ralph said. 'Elizabeth's got a day off, she's taken Martha out for a walk.'

Martha was my little sister. I went to peep in at baby William, who was sleeping in his crib. I did not kiss him for fear of waking him. It was so good to be back in our cottage where everything was within reach and in its right place. I never ever thought this crumbly little place would feel like home, but today it did. I felt like I'd been away for weeks and not only one night.

'Is there no bread?' I asked, looking into the empty cupboard, and turned to watch Ralph reply.

'There's no more flour,' he said. 'Last year's harvest wasn't enough to last us, and there's no money for grain to grind.' Ralph's hands were signing to me too, in a way that made him easy to understand. 'But Jacob's said he'll exchange some of our dried peas for corn,' he said.

'Glad to,' Jacob said. 'But things will be different now. Now we're following the Diggers way.'

'Aye. It's time. It can't come soon enough,' Ralph said. 'I swear, Mother will never go hungry again. That bailiff was here again this week, demanding our tithe. And I'll warrant it will go straight from the Fanshawes' bailiff to the King, like always. And from the King to his blasted Army to kill good honest men like my father. I'm telling you, when that bailiff showed his poxy face on our doorstep I nearly put my boot in his mouth.'

'Then it's a mercy someone was there to stop you.' Jacob said, laughing.

I agreed with Jacob, though I was too shy to join in the conversation. My brother had such a temper. Like milk waiting to boil over. Not that you'd guess it to look at him – with his angel face, his fair hair shining like gold. I paused in my thoughts to ladle ale into a tankard.

But he was unpredictable, as if two Ralphs lived in his skin side by side, and you never knew which Ralph you'd meet. Often he was on fire with some new enthusiasm, but other times he'd be bitter and morose. Once he'd nearly strangled a tinker man who'd cheated him of his change, and Elizabeth and I had to pull him away. But Ralph was always 'good Ralph' with us and never 'bad Ralph.'

Ralph and Jacob continued talking, poring over a printed pamphlet that was out on the table. I leant over Ralph's shoulder as I put down the beer and read the headline. 'A NEW-YEAR'S GIFT FOR THE PARLIAMENT AND ARMIE.' Further on, the word 'DIGGERS' appeared in big letters.

Another of Ralph's crazed ideas, no doubt.

How could I tell Ralph I wasn't going back to Markyate Manor?

Just then the door burst open and my older sister Elizabeth flew in. 'Ma not back?' she asked, untying her bonnet.

'Not yet,' Ralph said. 'You know Jacob, don't you?'

Elizabeth threw her ribboned bonnet down, revealing her curly hair, and gave him a cursory smile. I couldn't help but notice how Jacob's eyes lingered on her and it gave me a choking sensation in my throat.

'Is Martha outside?' Ralph asked.

Elizabeth nodded. 'Playing with the chickens.' She narrowed her eyes in my direction. 'What are you doing here?'

I didn't want to explain in front of Jacob and I could feel my face getting redder. The atmosphere thickened.

'I'll be going.' Jacob downed his beer in one long gulp. 'Till Sunday,' he said, already at the door. He turned to wave a hand at me,

'See if you can rally a few more for our cause, won't you?' Ralph said, 'We're going to give this world a good old shaking.'

'Aye, I will. If you think we've not had shaking enough.' Jacob said, then ducked away out of the door.

As soon as he'd gone Elizabeth stood in front of me, arms folded. 'The grand manor not suit you, then?' The smile that was trying to creep to her lips was only just under control.

I turned my head away. I wasn't going to listen to her taunts. I went to the window, stared out into the orchard, but she followed me, pushed her face in front of mine.

'I knew you wouldn't last two minutes. What did you do?'

'I haven't done anything.' But I knew my face told a different story. 'Go away!' I shouted, and turned my back to her.

But I knew Elizabeth would be talking to Ralph and sure enough when I turned back they were arguing with each other but looking at me.

'I suppose you'll let her get away with it again,' Elizabeth said, whispering, thinking I couldn't make out her words. 'Abi this, Abi that. It's always about her. She's deaf on purpose half the time.'

I cast her a cold look on my way out, and slammed the door so hard I was sure it would rattle the house. Curse Elizabeth. She'd no idea what it was like to be me. She should try it. See how she'd like it. Then she'd know what it was like to work so hard, and strain every minute just to be part of the conversation.

I picked my way through the bare trees of the orchard down to the chicken shed. The hens were all out, scratching in the dirt, fluffing their feathers, ignoring me. They'd always been my task.

Who'd fed them this morning,? I wondered. Not Elizabeth, the lazy fox.

Five minutes later Ralph came after me. I turned my back on him, but he took hold of my shoulder to bring me round.

'Pay no heed,' he said. 'She doesn't mean anything. She's jealous that's all. She wanted to go up to the big house herself. She's got this foolish idea that it's beneath her to be a serving maid to the apothecary. Even though they pay much more than the manor.'

'Let her go to the Manor then.'

'What is it? What's happened?' His pale blue eyes searched mine.

'I can't do it. It's hopeless. I can't understand them. The Cook doesn't open her mouth when she talks. Lady Katherine, well she's…she's just not what I expected.' I couldn't tell him, not even Ralph; that I'd nearly killed my mistress, or that I'd been such a clod as to try to polish spoons with duck paste.

'Did you give them notice?'

I shook my head miserably.

'Come on then, no harm done. I'll walk you back. Mother need never know.'

'I'm not going back.' I felt the words snap from my tongue.

A shadow crossed his face. 'Sure you are. You're a hard worker, they'll be glad to have you back. You were only gone from here one day and we missed your hands about the place - feeding the chickens and laying the fires.'

He was coaxing me, holding me by the elbow, and I knew how it worked with Ralph. He flattered people – always got his own way, he had a knack of smoothing everything over so it looked all spick and span when really it was all confusion underneath. He used the same tone when he'd done something bad and wanted to hide it.

'Remember when Mother took you round the village?'

I cringed. It was the most humiliating experience of my life. Mother thought if people could see how bright and willing I was, how good with my letters, that they'd take me on. Door to door we went, looking for an apprenticeship, or any sort of work, with Mother looking more desperate every minute. Every place we stopped they looked me up and down doubtfully, and every villager shook her head, until by the end I was so hunched and sullen that nobody would even look twice. I could have borne it all, except for their pity – that I could not endure.

Ralph squeezed my hand. 'It's hard for Mother with the two little ones since Father was killed. She despaired when nobody would give you a chance. And you wouldn't do that to her would you? Give up at the first try?'

I pictured the hopeful look on Mother's face, when we'd tried to find work, and the thought of it tugged at my heart. It was my fault we had lost everything and I just couldn't bear to think of failing her again. Ralph was right. It wouldn't be fair to give up so soon. After all, nobody else had ever offered me any sort of work.

I squared my chin and took a deep breath. 'But I didn't ask for leave.'

'A month's trial, that's what's usual,' Ralph said.

'What will they say, though when I go back?'

'Don't worry. I'll talk them round.' He squeezed my arm and I believed him. Things never looked so bad when my big brother was there. Before I knew it we were on the road and Ralph was talking, to keep me from thinking. He knew I had to keep watching his face and hands in case I missed anything.

'It will only be for a while anyway,' he said. 'In a few years we'll have our new Digger community running, and you can join with us. Once the trouble's died down. And I'm telling you, there's bound to be trouble.' It sounded as though he relished it.

'Wait.' I was breathless trying to keep up with his stride and to read his words as we walked.

We stopped then and leaned up against a wall. 'Tell me,' I said, 'Tell me again. I didn't understand it all. What trouble?'

'Some of us are settling on common land, ours by right. They call us the Diggers, because we'll dig the land ourselves and make our own living in service to no-one.'

'What land? You don't own any land, do you?'

'This land.' He stamped his feet up and down in the grass. 'God's land. We'll plough the common land that belongs to us all. Cultivate it and live from it. People have already tried it in Wycombe and in Iver, led by a man called Winstanley. I'm telling you, it's the only way forward. Jacob and I are going to see Winstanley next week.'

'But taking common land - doesn't that make you as bad as them? As bad as the landlord who takes our best grain, as bad as the Fanshawes?'

'No, you don't understand. Any of us can work it, that's the point. It's common land, for the common people.' He ran his hand through his hair, opened his eyes wide and spread out his arms as if he would blast me away with his idea. 'It belongs to us all, every man whatever his position in life. There'll be no buying or selling, no profiteering. Each man can take what he needs. Everything will be held in common.'

No buying or selling? I took a step back. I couldn't imagine it, that people could survive that way. Just the idea was frightening. How would they get soap, or linen, or laces if they didn't buy them? I pulled up a grass stalk, sucked on the sappy root. 'I can't think it will go down well with the Sheriff. Who will he tithe, if not us?'

Ralph shook his head at me in frustration. 'Look, it's a new idea, see? It's simple. We just share everything, work together for the common good. If someone has flour and another needs it, they can just help themselves.

Won't that be fine! They tried it on St George's Hill, Winstanley's men, but folk came and fired their houses. But fast as they tread us down we spring up again, like the corn.'

'And what about Jacob, is he for it?'

'He's right behind it.'

I let this sink in. If Jacob believed in it, it couldn't be all bad.

Ralph strode about, warming to his theme, 'There's about twenty of us, mostly young folk, but some older ones too that fought in the last skirmish for Parliament, ones that are forward-thinking. We're after building a new world. What's the point of Father dead on some field somewhere and all his fighting for nothing? If we don't take our land now, after fighting for it, what kind of men are we?'

I missed my father, though I could barely remember him, he'd been at war so often. I could remember the smell of him, the feeling of being held safe in his arms. But now he was lost. We'd heard reports of his death from his regiment.

I dragged my thoughts back to the conversation. 'But what about those who graze their sheep on the common land? Won't they object?' I said.

'Oh don't throw problems at it before it's begun.' Ralph sighed, 'They can still use it just the same. There's plenty of room for us all.'

'Can I come with you then, to the common, to see for myself?'

'See what they say at the house, they might not let you have the day off.'

His face told me he didn't want me there with his friends. I sighed. I'd probably do something stupid there, too. I should go back to Markyate Manor and Lady Katherine, try and do something right for once, make amends for the trouble I'd caused everyone. And I wanted to prove Elizabeth wrong. I'd see her laugh on the other side of her face when I'd earned enough to buy that plot of land for Mother.

Ralph set off ahead and I watched his purposeful strides as he loped along. Other men were jealous of Ralph's radiant good looks, the way he drew the women's eyes, and wherever he went, sure enough, trouble always followed. The Diggers was another of his fads, I knew, and it sounded like robbery to me, taking land that wasn't yours without anyone's say-so. My stomach pitched with fear for him. Anyone could see it was an idea that would find no favour with either Cromwell or the King. It could even be treason.

CHAPTER FOUR

Rule of Thumb

Mistress Binch was drawing water from the well. She stood up from cranking, watching us approach, hands on hips, face black as a storm cloud. And all the while my pace became slower, as I hid behind Ralph.

When we were close enough to hear she shouted, 'You needn't think you're coming back. Not after letting us down like that.'

Ralph smiled his winning smile at her. 'She just got a bit scared, it being her first day. She's sorry for causing any trouble, aren't you, Abi?'

I managed a nod.

Mistress Binch gabbled on. I caught the tail-end of the words, '.. someone reliable. I've got a party of noblemen and his Lordship coming tomorrow, and only me to get things done.'

Ralph just waited until she seemed to have run out of things to say. He smiled long and slow. 'Then you'll be wanting the extra help, and she's willing. She just needs to get used to you. It takes her time to get to see how you form the words, then she'll have no trouble reading you.'

Mistress Binch took a big breath as though she was going to say a lot, 'I don't know –'

'Now, where do you want it?' Ralph interrupted, picking up one of the pails that was brimming with water and indicating with his head for me to take the other.

'The scullery. Now wait a minute –'

Ralph was already moving towards the house. I followed, trying not to slop water over the edge. As we went up to the back door I caught sight of a figure at the window, a figure that retreated when it saw me look. Lady Katherine. I'd know her even from twenty paces, by the glint of her copper hair.

By the time we were indoors Ralph was conversing pleasantly with Mistress Binch, admiring two new loaves steaming on the griddle. Vegetables clagged with earth lay on the table, so I rolled up my sleeves. If I was going to stay, I'd better start and look useful. I took a basin and a brush and began to scrub. A few moments later Ralph tapped me on the arm to take his leave. He had a slice of warm bread in one hand, but we embraced and I saw Mistress Binch's face soften a little before it returned to its customary ill-temper.

Mistress Binch kept me busy the rest of the day with cleaning and chopping, and with plucking two geese for the next day's feast. There was so much to do I could hardly catch a breath. I scurried up and down corridors mopping and polishing, turning beds and beating drapes. So I did not set eyes on Lady Katherine until darkness fell.

After I'd set down the supper tray, Lady Katherine said, 'Who was that with you today, carrying a pail into the house? Nobody told me we had taken on any other servants.'

'My brother, milady.' I was reluctant to say more about why he was there.

'But he does not work here.'

'No milady. He's a farmer.' I did not tell her he used to be a gentleman.

'And where is that?' She toyed with the spoon, did not eat.

'In Wheathamstead village, milady, close by. We plough four acres.'

'He's very tall. And he has not your colouring.'

'He's got hair like my father. I take after Mother.'

'So what had he come for?'

'He came to see if I was settling in, m'lady, and he helped Mistress Binch bring in the water.' I blenched at this white lie, but could think of nothing else to say.

She raised her eyebrows as if the answer surprised her. 'Then he must be a kind young man to take the trouble. I'd like to meet him. Next time he calls, you will introduce us. Mistress Binch says we need more help on the estate with all our men away at the Wars, and I might be able to persuade Grice to take him on.'

'Yes milady.' She could go whistle. I wasn't bringing Ralph in here. He thought little enough of the Royalists, and I could not imagine him even in the same room as Lady Katherine. He was never good with authority, always had to kick up against it.

I turned away to fix the fire then, though I could sense her watching me still, by the hairs that prickled up on the back of my neck, as though she could read my thoughts.

That night I must have slept but it was still dark when I woke, my eyes searching desperately for any spark of light. My body seemed to hear things my ears did not. A glint of a star at the window drew me there and I put my face to the thick pane of glass.

Along the drive there were horses approaching. Men with pikes, a trundle cart. Their black shapes flooded together then separated. I did not know if they were roundheads or cavaliers, but I did know I did not want to be alone.

I lit a taper with shaking fingers and hurried down to shake Lady Katherine, who struggled to sit up in bed, clutching the sheets, her eyes wide. There was still a candle burning on her table and the fire was a red glow in the hearth.

'What's the matter?'

'Men, m'lady. Men and horses.'

She jumped out of bed and went to the window. 'It's my Lord. Quick, barricade the door.'

We dragged the large trunk across the entrance and locked the other door with a key. Lady Katherine obviously did not want me to go downstairs to open up to him, as a good servant should.

'He's hammering at the front door,' she said, stock still, hand pressed to the neck of her nightgown. In the half-light I could not tell if she was angry or afraid.

I started towards the door, but she grabbed me by my apron tail. 'No.'

Through my feet I felt a faint vibration. 'He's knocking,' I said, 'But if I don't go, I expect Mistress Binch will let them in.'

I could hear nothing, but saw my mistress startle and jump. 'They're in,' she said. 'They didn't wait. Just like last time. They've broken a window. They've been fighting so long, so much blood and battle, nothing matters to them. They can't be civilised men anymore.'

I saw her bite her lip then look to the door, 'Help me,' she said.

The house was full of odd vibrations, like footsteps, scuffling. Lady Katherine hurried to push against the trunk that held the door shut. I saw the door rattle and shiver in the jamb. The latch started to move up and down. Quick as a wink I grabbed the candle snuffer from the side table and pushed it into the hole under the tongue of the latch. Lady Katherine was surprisingly strong, she shoved on the trunk with all her might, and I held the snuffer pressed tight, our eyes locked silently on each other. Finally the movement of the door ceased.

Her green eyes flicked from side to side as she listened. 'They've gone back downstairs,' she mouthed, 'My stepfather has called for liquor and Mistress Binch is fetching them wine from the cellar.'

I nodded. She put her hand to her lips, in a gesture that we should be quiet.

She pulled the bolster and pillows from her bed, laid them out on the floor. She pointed to it, and I understood that was to be my bed that night.

She climbed back onto hers, but did not lie down. She clung on to the sheets, listening to what was happening below. I stared up at the ceiling, where cobwebs wavered in the moonlight. I could not sleep for fear. My heart jangled in my chest, I was ready to leap and run.

Curse Ralph. It was his fault I was back in this bedlam house with its crazy mistress and thuggish lord, who'd break into his own house, and whose own family barred the door against him. I thought of the weapons stashed in the room below. If only I'd thought to pick up a knife.

Right until the dawn we tossed and turned. When the light was enough to see by, I stood, began to lay out her clothes. They smelt of the cinnamon and rose that she used to sweeten them. As I shook out her skirts on the foot of the bed she said, 'The birds are singing. Mistress

Binch will be in the kitchen soon. We'd better wait a while before we go down.'

'Very good, milady.'

'When they come home after fighting it's best to leave them to become sober. My stepfather is no respecter of women, even at the best of times. To him I am simply my fortune, nothing more.'

'What about your husband? Will he not look to you?'

'That squab? No. He is barely a man. Thomas does whatever my stepfather tells him to do. Sir Simon cheated my mother out of her fortune, and now he'd cheat me by marrying me off to his nephew. He arranged our marriage when I was only fourteen. Do you know what day he chose for our wedding? April Fool's Day. What a jest.'

'Does Thomas treat you badly?' I thought of her words on the first night.

'He does not mean to. But he is a milksop. Too frightened of my stepfather to do anything but bleat. Come, you may dress me now.'

We went down to the great chamber together. Milady's eyes were dark-shadowed from lack of sleep, but she entered the room proudly with her head up and shoulders back. For the first time I felt sorry for her, entering this room where every man turned to stare.

A sea of eyes and beards met us. About fifteen cavaliers, in the King's livery, but dirty, their swords lying about their feet. The smell of them all packed so close together was like an over-ripe cheese. They were scraping out their bowls and downing ale from a motley collection of tankards.

Lady Katherine dipped a curtsey to a pale young man with long drooping curls and he bade her sit beside him. That must be Thomas, her husband. The older man on his other side ignored her, his florid red face almost hidden by supping from his bowl. From his position at the head of the table I guessed he was Sir Simon.

I couldn't help a twinge of disappointment. They were ugly, coarse-looking men.

The other soldiers watched Lady Katherine a moment, and some laughed and made obscene gestures at me, before going back to their bowls of gruel. I hastened red-faced to the kitchen to find Mistress Binch boiling eggs in a big pan. She let out a stream of angry words, and thrust a basket of bread at me. I hurried to deliver it to the table.

From then on I was kept busy fetching and carrying and avoiding men's paws until the men took to horse again with a great clatter. The great chamber was suddenly empty, but there was ale swabbed on the table and bread and mutton-grease trodden over the floor.

So no need to wonder how my morning would be spent. I ruefully collected the trenchers and plates, the knives and spoons, and began the washing.

In the course of the morning I learnt from Mistress Binch that Sir Simon and the Cavaliers had taken the weapons from the store-room and gone on to meet with the mysterious Grice at Luton town. They were making plans to join the King if he had been able to gather a bigger army in Scotland and move it south against Cromwell's New Model Army.

'Why do you think Grice wanted a deaf girl, heh?' Mistress Binch said. 'Because the Fanshawes are for the King, and we don't want you tittle-tattling back to the village about all the King's affairs, that's why.'

I ignored her and scrubbed harder at the plates.

Sir Thomas Fanshawe and Sir Simon, Lady Katherine's stepfather hadn't been at all what I'd imagined gentlemen to be before I came to the Manor; I'd thought they would be quiet and dignified, not the uncouth ruffians I'd seen at the morning table. So I was nervous about serving them the evening meal.

When I went up to dress Lady Katherine, she was fidgety whilst I plaited her hair into a knot at her nape and dressed her side-curls.

'Do you ever wish you had a different life, Chaplin?' she said.

'No, milady.'

She watched me tie on her sleeves. 'Liar. All servants wish they were born more highly.'

I pretended not to hear and finished her laces into a bow with a hard tug.

'I hate this pomp and show.' Lady Katherine brushed down her blue velvet skirt impatiently. 'What is it for?' Then, catching me staring, 'My stepfather wants to show Aunt Ann that he has me under his thumb. That I am an obedient wife to his cowardly son. I hate them both. And now they allow me only one manservant of my stepfather's choosing and a single maid. So I have Grice who is as dark and gloomy as the devil, and you, whom no-one else will have.' I did not answer her, though plenty came to mind, but tied on the other sleeve.

'Did you hear me? Don't you care? I have just insulted you and you say nothing?'

'It is not my place, milady. Besides, there is nothing to say.'

'Tush.' She sighed. 'I did not mean it. I am just so tired of it all. I wish I was a servant, free to come and go where I please. I have seen only the inside of these walls for a whole year. Thank goodness they left me Blaze. I think I would go mad if I couldn't ride, but I can only ride out at night or where I won't be seen. If my stepfather found out about it he would put a stop to my riding unchaperoned, so I don't tell him. But sometimes I long for a change,' she said wistfully. 'I'd give anything to ride out in the sunshine, go to market, see some real life.'

I spoke quietly, 'If you would loan me a horse, I could chaperone you.'

'You? Can you ride?'

'My brother taught me.'

'Ah, your brother.' She stopped talking and seemed to think a moment, but then she threw her looking-glass down on the bed and said, 'I still could not ride out to the town with you.'

I turned away stiffly. She obviously did not think me a good enough servant to be seen at her side.

A hand came on my arm to get my attention, 'It's a Parliament town. They know who I am and what my family stands for. There is no love for me there; it would not be safe. Thomas has told me what Parliament men would do to women like me.' I frowned, and turned away not wanting to accept it.

That evening Sir Simon was first to arrive at the table. A closer look at him revealed a large-bellied man with a bulbous nose and small darting eyes. He led in Lady Ann Fanshawe, his brother's wife, on his arm. She was finely-dressed in a black brocaded bodice and a kerchief clasped with a thistle shaped brooch. Pearl drop earrings dangled by her throat. The woman who sat down next to her never looked up from the table. She was wearing a nondescript shade of grey and had a servant's look about her, so I guessed she must be Lady Ann's companion.

Lady Ann peered at the banquet, pursing her mouth, though Mistress Binch had produced a meal to tempt the taste buds of a queen. Roast breast of goose in a pool of blackcurrant sauce, jugged hare in its savoury sage gravy, vegetables on their Staffordshire dishes. The smell of it all made my mouth water. Who would have thought it, to look at her skinny frame, that Mistress Binch could cook this way?

I tried not to stare at the guests as I refilled their drinking bowls and passed them their plates whilst Lady Katherine and her husband sat, looking everywhere but at each other. What an ill match, I thought. Sir Thomas Fanshawe almost seemed to fade away, he was so colourless.

I took my place near the door as Sir Simon mumbled the Grace into his beard. Sir Simon and Lady Ann helped themselves generously to the meal, but Lady Katherine and the servant took only small portions.

'This house is nothing but a millstone around your neck, Simon,' said Lady Ann, spearing a chunk of meat, 'and hardly well-situated.'

'But it's in a fine position here, close by the river for trade, wouldn't you say so, sir?' Thomas said, looking to his uncle for support.

'That wasn't what I meant.' Lady Ann said. 'I meant you are in enemy country. Too close to St Albans where Cromwell has his cronies. Tell him, Simon.'

'We are thinking of selling, Thomas.' Sir Simon said. I watched their lips more intently then, for if he was saying that the house was to be sold, I would be a maid with no position again, and I'd only just arrived.

'But the King may yet win, and then this house will serve us well,' Thomas said.

'Only if he can fund an army,' Sir Simon said, 'and he has drained us all – all of us fighting for the old regime. The King needs more mercenaries. We will have to sell property to raise cash.'

'But if this house is to go, where shall I live?' Thomas looked from his uncle to his aunt.

'Baysford, Ponsbourne. We have property enough. Take your choice.'

Thomas looked uncomfortable. Two red spots of colour had risen on Lady Katherine's cheeks. She put down her fork.

'But this is my home,' she said. 'It was my mother's house. Am I to have no say at all in the matter?'

Sir Simon took another drink from his bowl before turning lazily to her, 'It is your husband's house now. And you'll go where Thomas goes, naturally.'

'No. I won't permit you to sell it.'

'Permit?' Sir Simon laughed. 'You will do as he says; he is your lord and master.'

'Thomas?' Lady Katherine turned to him in appeal.

I watched the lacklustre Thomas squirm under the eye of his uncle. 'Well, I –'

'Of course, if there was a child to consider, then perhaps…' Sir Simon let the words hang.

'How dare you! There will be no heir.' Lady Katherine stood and threw down her napkin on the floor. She looked as angry as a hornet. 'I would not bring a child into this loveless house.'

Sir Simon was out of his seat in a moment and holding Katherine by the arm. 'Fetch the rod, Thomas.'

'But I —'

'I said, fetch the rod. A wife must obey her husband; that is what the law says.'

Thomas took a riding switch from its hooks over the fireplace and held it out to his uncle.

'No,' Sir Simon said, putting his hands behind his back, 'Not this time. You are man enough now, and she's your wife. You must do your duty.'

Lady Katherine began to struggle to escape her stepfather's grip. My eyes must have been wide with horror because Sir Simon's eyes turned to me.

'You.' It was a summons.

I stepped away until my back pressed hard against the wall.

'Come here.'

I had no choice but to obey.

'Unlace her.'

He had to repeat it before I knew what he was saying. My hands shook as I unthreaded the laces at her back until the fine transparent lawn of her chemise was visible.

Sir Thomas was standing away, nervous, unwilling to lift his hand.

'Strike, boy!'

Thomas brought the switch down tentatively on Lady Katherine's back.

'Harder. Do you want an obedient wife or not?'

Thomas hit her again. Lady Katherine did not flinch.

Sir Simon wrenched the stick from Thomas's hands and cut it down on milady's shoulders with an almighty blow. I felt it whistle past and saw the blood seep from underneath to stain her chemise.

Again and again Sir Simon brought it down. I looked imploringly at Thomas, who screwed up his eyes as if he did not want to see, until finally he put his hands over his ears and shouted, 'All right Uncle, I understand!'

Sir Simon gave one more heavy blow so that Lady Katherine sank to her knees. 'You are too lenient. That is how it should be done. It worked with both my wives and it will with yours.'

Sir Simon threw down the switch at Thomas's feet and strolled away. At the table Lady Ann was helping herself to more goose. Her plate, that had been full before was now empty. She had been eating all the time the master was beating Lady Katherine. Next to her, her maidservant wiped a tear from her cheek, but she did not look up. Lady Ann picked a bone from her teeth.

'Lace her again,' Sir Simon said to me.

I helped Lady Katherine struggle to her feet, closed the bodice gently, fastened it as loosely as I could. I could tell her knees were rigid under her skirts. When it was done she sat dazed in her chair, face white as plaster.

All this time my master Thomas looked down at the floor, his face pallid and dewed with sweat.

'We will sell.' Sir Simon said. His expression said the matter was closed.

The rest of the meal went by in a blur. When the meal was finished Lady Katherine begged permission to retire, and it was granted. I cleared the plates and went down into the kitchen.

'How did they like it?' Mistress Binch's eyes were bright and eager.

'Sir Simon beat Lady Katherine. It was terrible.'

'But my roast goose, did anyone remark on it?'

'I don't know. I don't care.' I saw Mistress Binch's face fall, but I couldn't bear to talk of the food. 'Have you any chickweed or coltsfoot? I have to go up to Lady Katherine, her back is bleeding.'

'In the cold cellar, back of the shelf. Don't waste it.' Mistress Binch glared at me sourly.

I knocked gently on the door and pushed, but it would not open. I called softly, 'It's me, milady, Abigail Chaplin.'

After a few moments the door opened a crack and I went inside. Lady Katherine walked stiffly, like a peg doll. She had taken off her bodice but her chemise was stuck to her back with blood.

'God in heaven,' I said. 'Sit down and I'll fetch water.'

I wet the chemise and peeled it from her back, then rubbed the coltsfoot balm over the welts, careful to avoid the broken skin. Lady Katherine pressed her lips tightly together until they were white but she did not cry out. It was a mess, and guiltily I saw the bruise was still there too.

I did as my mother had taught me, remembering the instructions in her book of recipes for physick and cookery. I brought my mistress a clean nightdress and when I saw her hands were trembling, I helped to fasten it.

'I'll stay by the door. You must rest.' I put the candle snuffer into the gap to wedge the latch shut again.

She spoke then but I did not catch it. 'Pardon, milady?'

'Will there be more scars?'

'I don't know. It looks bad right now, but it'll soon heal.'

'What was that stuff you put on it?'

'Coltsfoot.'

'Thank you...Abigail is it?'

'My friends call me Abi.' I don't know why I said that, perhaps because she looked like she had few who loved her.

'Abi then. Sir Simon may send my husband to me tonight, but I do not wish to see him.'

I was in awe. She had shed not a single tear. 'I understand.'

I took up vigil on the trunk before the door, but all seemed quiet. After a few moments Lady Katherine went to the window, drew back the drapes.

Her shoulders sank as she exhaled a long sigh. 'Lady Ann's carriage. She's gone.' And I saw her lips whisper, 'And I hope to high heaven she meets a highwayman or plunderers on the road.'

I picked up the blood-stained chemise from the floor in thumb and forefinger to put it with the laundry. 'How do you stand it?' I asked. My father had struck me on the hand occasionally when I had forgotten my Bible verses, but nothing like this.

'You should not be asking. It's impertinent.' A moment passed between us, and then she said, 'I'm sorry. I forget myself. You were offering me your friendship, not your opinion.'

'It's alright milady, it must hurt.'

'You seem to understand everything I say,' she said. 'Are you completely without hearing?'

'Yes m'lady. I read lips and faces. You have good clear lips for reading. Sometimes it is hard though, when the words and the face say different things.'

'You speak well. I saw a deaf child once and she could hardly speak, only mumble.'

'I learned to speak before I lost my hearing, so I can remember what words sound like and the feel of them on my tongue.'

'Oh. I imagined you'd been born that way. What happened?'

She came and sat down opposite me, keeping her shoulders away from the back of the chair. Her eyes were interested, curious.

Usually I didn't like to talk about it, it was too private and too painful. But I was sorry for my new mistress. I gave her a defiant look to prove I did not really care. Tried to keep my voice offhand. 'It was the spotted sickness, the messels. Everyone in my family had it, everyone in the cottages, but I had it the worst.'

'Why? What was it like?'

'I had dreams, visions, as though my thoughts were on fire and running here and there where I couldn't catch them. When it was over, then I ...' Words would not come. Emotion threatened to overwhelm me. I looked down, concentrated on my feet in their stout working boots. Keeping my eyes down was my way of cutting off communication.

And I did not want to tell her about the spell, and the fire, about why I had deserved what had happened to me.

When I finally lifted my head it was to see her gaze still fixed on me. 'That must have been hard. How old were you?'

I swallowed, felt tears well up, but tossed my head. 'Nine.'

The word felt like a croak.

She stood up, winced. 'We have both had hardships to endure, I see. So I am glad to have you as my maid-servant, but I'm sorry, your days with me might be short. They are selling this house and there is little I can do. My step-father is not a man you can reason with.'

Was my employment to be so brief? I'd hardly earned anything yet. A few days' wages wouldn't buy anything. I wanted to save enough to buy that extra plot of land Mother wanted so much. And what would I do then, with no prospect of work? I did not relish the idea of following my brother into his digging venture either. Though I might be able to bear it if Jacob Mallinson was there.

A tap on my arm. 'You may help me with my hair, now.'

I flushed, I had been thinking of Jacob, instead of paying attention.

CHAPTER FIVE

A Disguise

'Lace me tight. I will not give them the satisfaction of thinking they have hurt me.'

In the morning Lady Katherine's back was beginning to scab and looked more angry and painful than ever, but she refused to be cowed. I admired her. She acted the lady. If I was her I'd have been too much in pain. She picked her way downstairs, but as we went I saw that several more paintings had been removed from their places.

'The paintings from the hallway,' Lady Katherine said to Thomas. 'Where are they?'

Thomas shifted his eyes to Sir Simon who was too busy wiping out his breakfast plate to notice. 'Lady Ann has taken them for safe-keeping.'

'You mean they've gone to fund troops for the King.' Lady Katherine persisted.

Sir Simon looked up.

'You watch your tongue, girl. I would have thought you'd had enough of a birching already.'

Later Sir Simon informed Lady Katherine a messenger had been and that they were riding out on urgent Royalist business. They would not be returning until after sunset. I was to tell Mistress Binch to arrange supper for their return. I let out a trembling breath as I watched Sir Simon swagger from the room with Thomas following limply, his hose sagging at the ankles. I was glad they were going, it felt as though we were all walking on thin ice when they were in the house.

'Count the silver spoons,' Lady Katherine said as soon as they'd ridden away.

The drawers were empty, and the display of pewter was gone too. I went to the kitchen to ask Mistress Binch if the Lady Ann had taken them.

'I don't know,' Mistress Binch said. 'But if they are gone I expect so. This house will be closed up soon, I can feel it. They're running everything down, and soon there'll be no place for the likes of us.'

'What will you do?' I asked.

'You and your questions. Leave off with them all.' But then she softened. 'I'm after being taken on by Lady Ann. She knows how a house should be run, not like Lady Katherine. No, Lady Ann keeps her house well in order even though Sir Richard is away. I've heard she can always get sugarloaf and spices for her kitchen, not like here where I have to scrimp just to buy a few herbs. Did Lady Ann say anything about my food?'

'No, but she did eat a second helping of everything.'

Mistress Binch was appeased, and nodded. 'Of course I don't know if she'd be prepared to take on the likes of you,' she said doubtfully. 'She'll want everything done right.'

I knew I would never want to work for Lady Ann. I didn't like her and suspected she'd be a tyrant of a mistress. But I supposed I'd have no choice if she offered me a place. I could not pick and choose as other girls did.

That day the men did not return and it made Mistress Binch short-tempered. She kept me hard at it with the besom and scrubbing brush. The house was filthy and I was determined I would scrub it top to bottom, get rid of the cobwebs and have everything sparkling. I worked like a demon, until my hands were red raw with scrubbing, but at least when the overseer, Mr Grice, came, he could not say I wasn't earning my keep. Who knows, he might even give me an extra shilling.

I tended my mistress's back at night with more salves and ointments, though I cursed her because there was so much to do. I felt like saying, I could do with that ointment myself, for my sore hands.

Still no news from the men, until one day in the following week a messenger came with a letter for my mistress.

I was just sprinkling the new rushes in the main chamber with dried lavender when Lady Katherine appeared, waving the vellum in her hand.

'It's going badly for the King, so my husband and my step-father are going away. France, probably. That's where they went last time. He'll write again, but Thomas says it will be at least a week.'

Oh no. Another week with no wages. Nobody had paid me anything yet.

My mistress did not notice my expression. She was brighter, like a different person. 'A whole week! You can keep me company. It is dull riding around the grounds and the woods all by myself. Thomas never offers to accompany me. And partly I am glad, for I dislike my step-father.'

Dislike. A strange word to give to someone who had beaten her so badly.

I realised then that the real gentry do not speak as we do, that their words are hedged-in with politeness. I picked up the tray and began to load it with her greasy breakfast plates.

'I suppose we could walk,' I ventured, 'around the grounds.' Anything to get away from the mop and bucket.

She grimaced. 'That's dull. I'd rather ride in the woods. I love the feeling of the wind, the speed, the pounding hooves. You could ride with me if I can find another horse and Binch could spare you. You'll need a cloak if it's wet.' She looked at me a moment and then said, 'Wait. I have an idea. Have you another cloak?'

'No milady.' As if I'd have extra clothes just hanging about, on my pay.

'Then a skirt, bodice? Her eyes were all lit up with excitement.

I caught on to what she was saying and began to protest, 'No, I don't think –'

'We can be two servant girls out for a stroll. It's market day tomorrow in Wheathamstead.'

I forgot myself and said, 'They'll recognise you straight away. Look at you, all that fiery hair.'

'Haven't you a coif, or a hood I can wear?'

'Only this kitchen one, and it smells of woodsmoke.'

She smiled, 'Even better if I smell like a servant. You will give me your coif, and I will come to your room to see what else you have.'

'But –'

'It's an order.' She held out her hand.

I untied it and handed it over. I felt suddenly naked without it, with my dark hair all showing. Our eyes locked a moment. A moment ago I had fancied we were almost friends, but there was no mistaking who was the mistress now.

I bobbed a curtsey and marched away with the tray.

In the kitchen Mistress Binch was sour at me because I wasn't wearing my cap and because I was not helping enough in the kitchen. She wanted a kitchen maid, and

Lady Katherine wanted a lady's maid, and somehow I was to cut myself in two and be both.

When I told Mistress Binch I was to walk out with Lady Katherine the morrow and we'd be gone the whole afternoon, she said, 'Where? His Lordship says she's not to go wandering about.'

'Just in the grounds, she wants to paint some flowers.'

Mistress Binch spouted a torrent of angry words at me but I pretended not to hear and turned my back. That was until an iron ladle hit me on the shoulder. I grabbed the bucket of corn for the chickens and banged the door behind me, before she could throw something else.

I scattered the corn half-heartedly. There was a prickling sensation in my stomach. Deceit always gave me such a feeling because I knew it was a sin and that it always came back to bite you in the end. I could not disobey Lady Katherine, yet my heart knew that pretending to be something you were not was a dangerous idea. Especially if you were Lady Katherine Fanshawe pretending to be a Parliament maidservant.

CHAPTER SIX

A New Arrival

The next day I hadn't time to dwell on the afternoon's outing because as I was scouring the pans Mistress Binch burst in from outside. 'Mr Grice is coming. Quick. Run and put on a clean apron. Then to the hall.'

Her face was anxious, so I shot up the servant stairs and gave myself a hasty splash in the water bowl and slicked my hair back. As I went down the stairs I glanced out of the window and saw a tall figure riding towards the house at a brisk trot. He had a pale clean-shaven face under his steeple hat, his hands were white and gloveless on the reins. Behind him on two heavy hunters followed men in dark livery, a packhorse trotting between them.

By the time I got to the hall Mistress Binch was there smoothing her apron and brushing down her sleeves. A moment later she heard the bell and rushed forward to open the door. It had no sooner widened a crack than Mr Grice was already through, leaning on a stick, his eyes casting about. The two servants followed. They were tall, thick-set men with the bored manner of hired men. Mr Grice's eyes settled on me.

He inspected me from a distance. 'The new maid, is it?' he asked Mistress Binch.

'Yes Sir.'

'She's not wearing a cap. Make sure she wears one in future.' He came over and examined me, lifting my chin as if he would inspect the cleanliness of my neck. 'Is she any use?'

Mistress Binch nodded, her desire to please Mr Grice over-riding her usual bad temper.

'Tell her to fetch my saddlebags in from the stables and bring me some ale. My men will unload my other luggage.'

I stared because I couldn't help it. His eyes were slightly protruding, as was his lower lip, his skin was smooth as wax. His mouth opened and closed like a fish.

Mistress Binch prompted me and I ran to fetch the bags from his horse which was a rangy black gelding with an ill-tempered expression. When I hauled the saddlebags over my arm, I almost fell over, they were so heavy. No wonder, one of them gaped open to reveal a travelling Bible and some other large leather-bound books.

Mr Grice beckoned me forward and set off up the stairs expecting me to follow. He knew exactly where to go, so all I had to do was keep up with his limping gait, and he moved very quickly for a man with a wooden foot. Up the stairs he went, with a practised swing, with me panting behind him, out of breath from carrying his heavy panniers. On the landing he paused, put a forefinger to one of the empty patches where paintings had hung, shook his head, then led me to the west wing and into a guest chamber.

'There.' he said, pointing to the floor. I let the bags fall where he pointed. Just beneath the bed I saw a mouse-trap with a half-decomposed mouse. He saw me look, wrinkled his nose at the odour. 'You will empty all the traps.' He went on with more instructions, which could have been, 'bring fresh linen,' and what looked like 'juggle you.'

I just stared. Something about him disconcerted me.

'Do you understand? A jug and ewer.'

Ah. Now I understood. He approached very near, and looked straight into my eyes. 'If Lady Katherine gets letters from her husband or Sir Simon Fanshawe they are to come to me first.'

I didn't know what to say. It seemed dishonest somehow to Lady Katherine to interfere with her correspondence.

He took a step even closer, frowning. His breath smelt faintly of scurf and decay. 'Are you dumb? Did you understand? She demanded a maid, and I agreed to your employment ...' His mouth pronounced the words carefully, '... but it can be stopped just as easily.'

I swallowed, struck dumb. Not because of his words, but because his eyes were cold as marble.

'Come here each evening after prayers, to bring me her letters. Anything that goes in or out of the house.'

Still I stood staring, until his hand grabbed my wrist, jerked it hard. I recoiled but he held it fast. A stinging slap on my cheek that made me gasp.

'My leg needs dressing every day. You will bring water and brandy and linen bandages.' He pointed to his foot.

When I did not reply I saw him shake his head and spit out something insulting that looked like 'imbecile girl'.

'You are dismissed,' he snapped at me.

I fled out of the door, my cheek burning, and took in a great breath of air. He thought I was stupid, but I was just nervous. There was something ruthless as a hawk about him. Lady Katherine, well she was demanding enough, but I sensed Mr Grice was of another mould altogether.

Terrified of bringing down more wrath from Mr Grice, I ran down to the kitchen for a shovel and a sack to empty the mouse traps then went into all the rooms on my grisly task. I could hardly bear it, seeing the small dismembered bodies. As I went, I wished I could hear, because the sound of Grice's walking would tell me where he was and I was frightened he might suddenly loom up behind me.

In the kitchen I asked Mistress Binch what to do with the sack.

'Throw them out the back, near the midden. We need another cat. But Henshaw, the maid who was here before you, wouldn't have one in the house. Said they made her sneeze.'

'Where can I get one?'

She raised her eyebrows to the ceiling. 'They're everywhere. Are you blind as well as deaf? In the stableyard and barns. One of the farm cats has just had a litter. See if you can persuade one inside. As long as you keep it out from under my feet, mind. I'll be busy now with Mr Grice and his serving men to feed. And for heaven's sake, get that sack out of here, it stinks.'

Afterwards I went to my mistress. She was sitting by the window with an embroidery frame on her lap. 'A letter came from Thomas first thing this morning,' she said. 'Before Grice arrived. Thomas apologised to me. For the last…unpleasantness. They have gone to France for a while, to rally support for the King from the French court. He says he'll write soon about who will look to me whilst he is away.'

'That's good.'

'Strange, the letter must have been delayed, as Mr Grice is already here. I expect he will be in charge as usual until they return, and who knows how long that might be?' She stabbed at the embroidery with her needle, leaving pinprick holes in the linen. 'I don't understand him. Mr Grice seems very ill-tempered all of a sudden, and I don't like the look of his serving men. I've never met them before and they look like rough brutes.'

I agreed with her, though it wasn't my place to say so.

'Mr Grice says Thomas has forbidden me to ride out or leave the grounds,' she went on. 'Or rather Sir Simon has. I expect Thomas just agrees with whatever my stepfather says like always. Grice says I've to spend my time on Bible studies.' She made a sour face. 'I thought that was over, my instruction from Grice. But you haven't forgotten, have you? That we're going out to the market tomorrow?'

'But what about Mr Grice? You just said, he's forbidden you to ride.'

'We'll have to find a way past him. I'll think of something.'

The doubt must have shown in my face. I'd seen enough of him to know he wasn't a man I wanted to cross.

'It might be dangerous, m'lady. You said yourself, it's a Parliament town.'

'Not if I'm well-disguised. And stop looking like that. You'll do as I say. I'll come to your room after the mid-day meal.

That night I brought water as Grice asked, and he made me change the dressing on the stump of his leg. It was a fearful wound, only half-healed. I wondered how he could stand the pain of it. His wooden foot with all its straps was leant up against the wall. I would have felt sorrier for him, but he scared me, and just the sight of it made me gag.

When I came out of his room with my bowl of water and soiled strips of muslin I felt as though I should wash my hands; not from the wound but because it seemed some dirty business was lurking just under the surface. Grice and his men made me uneasy. They were men designed for fighting, not for taking care of two half-grown women in an abandoned house.

CHAPTER SEVEN

The Stocks

When I first saw Lady Katherine in my clothes I could only stare. She did not look like Lady Katherine at all with her face scrubbed pink and her hair braided flat under my kitchen cap. Out of her heeled slippers we were almost the same height, she just an inch taller. She had put on boots, but they were shiny and new.

'Do I look like a servant?' she asked me. She twirled around, held up her skirts.

'No,' I lied, 'you look like a lady dressed in servant's clothes.'

'Spoilsport. It is no use protesting. We are going out, and I expect you to behave as if I'm a servant to all we meet.'

'Then I hope we will meet no-one.'

'I intend to meet someone, because we are going to market to buy a horse.'

I gaped at her then.

'If we buy a horse then you can ride out with me.'

I said nothing, but worried that it would seem odd, a servant buying a horse. And what would happen to us if anyone found out she was Lady Katherine? They would think she'd come to spy. Tempers were hot since the Royalists came through and plundered the town. I'd seen grown men weep at the loss of their hard-earned life savings, their harvests and their livestock. Horses were scarce and anyone showing too much wealth suspicious.

'How will we get past Mr Grice?' I asked. The sight of her in servant clothes made me bold.

'I told him some of the fences were down. Deer. He's going to take his men and ride out to inspect them.'

We hurried down the servants' stairs and out of the front door, with me looking like a shifty fox to left and right in case Mr Grice or Mistress Binch should appear. As we passed the walled garden Mr Grice and his two dark-clad servants trotted past. I moved like quicksilver, pulled her ladyship down behind the garden wall.

She giggled, which made me angry. I tugged her round the edge of the vegetable plot and into the adjoining woodland, but then, realising what I was doing, let go of her arm as if it was red hot. I should not have even touched her ladyship at all, I knew, it was too familiar to touch her without permission. I wiped my hand down my skirt feeling guilty.

Once in the woods I breathed a sigh of relief. How strange it was, to be leading the way with my mistress

following behind me. When I turned to look, for an instant I thought she was Elizabeth and I had to remind
myself to tread carefully, keep watch. It wasn't only
Grice I was worried about, but the whole village. They'd
blame me if they found out who my companion really
was.

The sun was peeping through the clouds and the
hems of our skirts picked up the remaining dew in the
shadows, melting it into dark stains. We walked the few
miles briskly, down the coffin route and over the stiles.
We avoided the main highway which was preyed upon
by footpads and thieves. I was anxious for the outing to
be over as soon as possible.

The town square was set out with trestles and the straw-
littered pens in the meat market gave off a pungent odour
of dung. I crossed my fingers tightly. Pray God we
would not meet anyone who might know my mistress.
My eyes darted here and there searching people's faces
for the tell-tale flicker of recognition. As we approached
I saw some horses tethered, and I pointed, but Lady
Katherine ignored me, she was strolling over to a stall
stocked with jars of honey and preserves.

Horrified, I ran to grab hold of her arm and pulled her
away. 'Don't speak,' I whispered as she took a purse
from round her neck, about to ask the price. 'Please –
don't speak. I'm afraid your manner of speech will give
you away.'

I saw the realisation dawn in her eyes.

'I'll buy for you,' I said, 'if you tell me what you want. Most of them know me.'

'Very well. I understand. I have only a little money, but I'll ask you to make the purchases.'

I followed close on her heels as she browsed among the stalls. I saw a man on one of the trestles watch with suspicion as she stroked some kidskin gloves, and then move towards her as she picked up some yellow-dyed silk ones.

I nudged and frowned at her and shook my head. Serving girls such as us would not even dare to pick up such items as they would be well beyond our purse. She dropped them and moved on, a red flush on her cheeks. Unable to bear it much more I said, 'Come on,' and guided her over to where the horses were tied. Before I could prevent her, she bent and skilfully felt down the legs of a grey mare, looked in the mouth of a tired-looking bay.

The owner of the bay, a drover in a wide-brimmed soft hat, rushed over. 'You looking for a cart horse? This one's got a good few years in him yet.'

'No, a riding horse.' The words were out of her mouth before I could stop her.

The man stared at her, but she stared back. In a maidservant this looked brazen and I could see his annoyance rise before he tempered it.

'My son might have something for you then,' he said. 'Soper's the name, John Soper. Hey, Ned, over here!'

The son ambled over dragging a sad-looking roan pony by the headcollar. It was about fourteen hands tall and so thin that its ribs showed.

Lady Katherine began to shake her head, but I felt sorry for it and said, 'Yes. How much?'

'Four shilling.'

'No. That's robbery.' Lady Katherine would not be silent. 'He's an ill-fed animal and we'll pay no more than two.'

The son's mouth dropped open, but the father frowned and drew himself tall. 'Who are you to accuse my son of ill-treating his horse?'

'Come away,' I said to my mistress, pulling at her sleeve. I could feel trouble in the air as surely as I could feel the coming rain.

But she was angry now, and retorted, 'A maid who will not be cheated. Two shilling, he's worth.'

'The devil he is! Who is your master? I'll have words to say to him.'

'Lady Katherine Fanshawe, and she'll have words to say to you in return.'

I was aghast. I looked from one to the other.

'That nest of fawning scoundrels? I wouldn't even spit on them.'

'It is you who are the scoundrel,' Lady Katherine said.

'You'd cheek me? A slip of a servant girl? A few hours in the stocks should calm you down.' He lunged and caught hold of Lady Katherine by the arm.

'No,' I cried, as the son took hold of my arm in a grip like iron tongs, 'she was jesting. She didn't mean anything. Let us go, we'll go peaceful now.'

But they began to drag us away towards the stocks. I kept on calling apologies, but they were too strong and would not listen or leave go. Ahead of me Lady Katherine dug in her heels and I hoped no-one but me had noticed the quality of her boots as they scraped furrows in the dirt.

Soper stuck out a foot and tripped my mistress so she staggered and fell. He manhandled her into the stocks first. Her eyes were wide with shock. Ned pushed down on my shoulders, but I kicked out. A satisfying jolt as my heel hit his shin. His palm flashed out and stung my cheek.

A large figure loomed between us and grabbed Ned by the collar, almost lifted him off his feet. His mouth opened in a yelp and he let go. Ralph tightened his grip on Ned, twisting until he choked. I almost wept with relief. But then I realised. Ralph would want to know who I was with. It was a disaster.

'What's going on here?' Ralph said. 'Abi?'

Soper squared up to him, 'This maid was rude to me, she's got a mouth on her that needs stopping. We're letting her cool off in the stocks.'

'Now wait a minute; that seems a bit rough,' Ralph said, 'I don't know this maid, but this is my sister, Abigail.'

'Your sister? Well, I don't think much of the company she keeps.'

'And I don't think much of a man who'll pick on two serving maids for nothing at all.'

Ralph's face was growing hotter and I knew where this would lead.

'Ralph,' I tugged at his sleeve.

Ralph looked down at my imploring face. He took a deep breath, unclenched his hands. With a great effort he said, 'Leave the maid be, Soper. I dare say she meant no harm.'

'She cheeked me.'

'Does your son never cheek you?'

Soper looked sheepish, glanced at Ned who had let go of me and was staring at us all.

'Aye. Well, maybe.' Soper loosened his grip and Lady Katherine managed to free herself and stand up. She had the sense to keep quiet this time, though her face was white and shocked.

I squeezed Ralph's arm and he looked down at me. 'It's alright, Abi,' he said. 'I've seen sense. I'm not going to leather him.'

Ralph looked pointedly to Lady Katherine.

'I didn't mean to cause offence,' she said quietly, head bowed down.

'There, then.' Ralph said, 'There's your apology.' He clapped Soper on the back. 'Let's fight for something worth our time, shall we? Like a future we can believe in.' I saw the anger seep from Soper's face but it was replaced with a look of suspicion.

'The Diggers, you mean? I heard someone say you'd gone over to them. Didn't they mutiny against Cromwell?'

'No,' Ralph said, annoyed. 'Those were the Levellers.'

'All these sects. I don't know what to make of them all. Waste of time, most of them. Or cowards.'

'There's nothing cowardly about the Diggers,' Ralph said.

'I'll take a look. Not promising I'll join or anything, but I'll take a look.'

'You, young Ned?' Ralph looked to the son.

The son glanced to his father who gave a barely visible nod.

Their reluctance was written all over their faces, but Ralph did not seem to notice. 'We'll meet here then,' he said, 'at seven bells on Sunday.'

He shook Soper's hand, whilst I brushed down my skirts and dare not look at my mistress who was still standing looking at the ground like a simpleton.

Ralph beckoned, 'Now Abigail, leave these good people alone, and come along with me. Bring your friend.'

Ralph strode away, but as we went I saw Soper raise his horned fist behind Ralph in a gesture of contempt, but I kept that to myself. We were in trouble enough already. I put my head down and we followed Ralph to the edge of the town where we could shelter under the eaves of a tithe barn from the oncoming drizzle.

'Now - you'd better introduce me,' Ralph said.

I did not know what to say so I let my eyes shift away.

'What's the matter? Are they treating you badly at the house?' his eyes sharpened with concern.

'No, they treat us well.' Lady Katherine said.

'We haven't met,' Ralph said, 'tell me your name.'

'It's Kate.'

'Pleased to make your acquaintance, Kate. I didn't realise Lady Katherine had any other maidservants.'

'I'm new,' Lady Katherine said, smiling at him. 'And you're Ralph. Abi's spoken of you.' I glared at her and she stopped talking.

'You're not from round here,' Ralph said, 'I can tell by your speech. Where are you from?'

Lady Katherine looked at me uncertainly.

'Devon,' I said. It was the first thing that came into my head.

'I bid you welcome, then. Take no notice of old John Soper, he's known for his short temper.' I marvelled at the pot calling the kettle black. 'What did you say to him?'

'Nothing.' I said, 'We just came to get a few provisions. We have to hurry back now. Lady Katherine will be waiting,' I said with a barbed look at my companion.

'Then I hope we will meet again, Kate.' Ralph raised his hat politely at my mistress, and she smiled back at him, swaying back and forth on her heels.

'Thank you,' she said, through lowered eyelashes, 'you saved me from disgrace.'

Ralph said, 'It was nothing,' but he smiled in a sheepish, pleased-with-himself way.

After he had gone I took her firmly by the arm. 'We're going back,' I hissed in her ear, almost dragging her away.

Once we were in open fields she stopped. 'We'd better hurry,' she said, grinning. 'Our mistress will be waiting.'

My heart had only just stopped hammering in my chest. 'How could you? I told you not to speak?' I was white hot with anger. 'Do you know what they'll do to you if they find out who you are?'

She put her hands on her hips and laughed. 'I haven't had so much merriment in years.'

I looked at her laughing and my mouth began to twitch. A bubble of laughter threatened to dispel my anger, though I tried as hard as I could to keep hold of my outrage. She saw and laughed harder, and finally I gave in. Soon we were both clutching our sides, helpless with mirth.

When we'd recovered she said, 'We didn't get a horse.'

'No,' I said, wiping my eyes, 'And we're not going to get one.'

'I keep thinking what Sir Simon would have done to Soper if he'd put me in the stocks!'

'Don't.'

'If it hadn't been for Ralph, I don't think we could have stopped them. He's very fine-looking, isn't he?'

'He's all right. Come on.' I did not like her talking of Ralph in such a familiar way. I set off across the common, did not turn to see if she was behind me. When we got to the high wall I stopped. She was a hundred paces behind and dragging her feet. I waited.

'I don't want to go back,' she said.

I tugged on the strings of my cap, unsure what to do. I couldn't make her, she was my mistress, but there was no doubt in my mind that she would have to. This sudden change in the order of things perplexed us both. I watched her face as she weighed her choices, saw her face harden.

'We will go in,' she said, 'but you will lend me your clothes again.' The mistress was back. Her whole manner had changed.

'Yes milady,' I said.

CHAPTER EIGHT

Nomansland Common

To my relief Mr Grice and his men, Pitman and Rigg, had spent the last two days inspecting the tenants and their cottages. I was glad he was away from the house, so I could walk the corridors without looking over my shoulder. When I went to dust his room, I saw that there were inventories laid out on the desk of all the tenants' cottages and their value. I scanned down the list until I saw my mother's house and land. Four pounds, the land was worth. I had no idea it was so much. How would I ever save all that? I'd have to work for years and years, and I didn't think I could stand it, not now Grice was here. Mistress Binch and Lady Katherine were bad enough. And I hadn't liked the way she'd looked at my brother, it gave me an uneasy feeling.

I wiped the duster over the washstand, but when I got to the desk there was a sheet of parchment with Sir Simon Fanshawe's signature on it. He'd signed it several times. And then I realised − it wasn't his signature. The ones at the top were more like Mr Grice's writing. Mr Grice was copying Sir Simon's signature. Why?

I had no time to think because when I took the document over to the window to look at it more closely I saw Ralph. He was walking up behind the house, bold as brass, shirt unlaced at the neck, and leading that roan pony from the market with him. Hurriedly, I put the paper back and ran down the stairs to the servant's door, curious as to what was going on.

'John Soper tells me Kate was trying to buy this pony.'

I frowned, but he continued to smile.

'So I persuaded him to part with it. He wasn't keen - in fact he was damned awkward - but I bartered for it. He wanted some of my lambs when they come, so we struck a bargain. Is she here?'

'Yes. I mean, no. It's her day off.' It was the first thing I could think of.

'Oh.' I could tell he was disappointed, and I was squirming in my shoes. I went to stroke the pony, which blew in my hand and rubbed his face against my side.

'He needs a bit of feeding, but I'll take him round to the stalls shall I?' Ralph said.

'No, I mean I think Milady's changed her mind about Kate having a horse. It was a foolish idea of hers; that one of us could ride out with her. And Mr Grice, he's a sour old stick, and I don't think he'll approve.' The pony seemed to read my thoughts and rubbed harder against my back.

'Oh. Well, I'll leave him anyway. He's a docile beast. No trouble. John Soper said Kate drove him a hard bargain, so I'd like her to look at him at least. If it's for her, she won't need to pay me. She can do me a favour sometime instead. But if your Mistress will pay, so much the better.'

'She won't. You'd better take him back.' I scuffed my shoe in the dirt. It was an expensive gesture, and not the sort of thing Ralph usually did. It was unlike him to give away his good livestock like that, and it bothered me.

'Why are you so flush all of a sudden?' I asked.

'We're giving up our goods. Ready for a Digger's life when we'll share everything. I thought it would be nice to start sharing right away.'

'Oh.'

'What's the matter?' Ralph said, 'You look like dog that's lost his bone.'

'Nothing. Just tired.' Up at the window the pale oval of Lady Katherine's face was just visible. I looked away sharply in case Ralph should see her.

'Lady Katherine must be working you both hard. Is there a chance she'll let you take some time off on Sunday?'

'I don't know. I can ask.' She owed me something, anyway.

'We're going to the Diggers. You were asking me what it's all about. Meet us earlier, after six bells, so we know you're coming. You can both come. Bring Kate too.'

Only last week he didn't want me there at all, now suddenly he was inviting me. Or rather he was inviting Kate. I dug in my heels. 'No. I mean, I might be able to, but Mistress probably won't let us both have the day off.'

'Shame. Kate's got no folks round here. It must be lonely.'

I didn't respond. He drew me tight and hugged me as if to brace me up. As he pulled away to go, he said, 'I know you don't like it at the Manor, but you'll soon get used to it. And it's good to know you're settled whilst we're getting our Digger community running.'

'What about Mother? Will she join you on the common?'

'No. She's old-fashioned, she's used to her little cottage and being tied to the big house. She's been a tenant of the Fanshawes ever since... since we lost our house. I've tried and tried to make her see that a new world is coming, but she just clings to the old ways. She doesn't hold with what I'm doing, but she'll not stop me. She knows I'm set on it.'

When he'd gone I waved at his back for a long while, the pony's lead in my hand. It had felt awkward lying to

Ralph about my mistress. All of a sudden I needed to watch every word I spoke. The pony nuzzled me again with sad eyes. The poor thing, he looked more confused than I did. I led him round to one of the vacant stalls and found him some hay. I could swear he almost smiled. His ears went forward and he was soon happily munching.

'You're a fine lad,' I said, patting him on the neck, 'If you were mine, I'd call you 'Pepper' because of your speckled coat, and I'd feed you on linseed and corn.'

But whether he was mine or not, I could see that now he was here I'd have to explain him to Mr Grice. Worse, I might have to ride out again with Lady Katherine, and who knows what trouble that might lead to?

I sighed, wished life was not so complicated. All I wanted was a simple maidservant's position with a decent wage. And so far, the whole household was mad as bedlam, and nobody had paid me so much as a bean. I watched as Pepper carried on chomping and when one of the stable lads came, I headed back to the house where I knew Mistress Binch would be waiting, wondering where I'd got to. And as for Lady Katherine, I was sure she'd be full of questions. She seemed to have a sixth sense as far as my brother was concerned, always at the window when he appeared.

Sure enough, the call came later in the afternoon whilst I was winding the handle on the butter churn. A hand clapped on my shoulder and startled me. 'Lady Kathe-rine wants you,' Mistress Binch said. She sniffed, 'I've got better things to do than chase round after you, you know.'

I heard her loud and clear. I'd got used to the way she formed her words now. I bobbed a curtsey and hurried in the house to the big chamber.

Lady Katherine was back to her stiff manner, stitch-ing a cushion cover, sitting upright in her boned bodice and petticoats. 'Your brother was here,' she said, 'I saw him out of the window. And he brought that horse. It was the same one, wasn't it?'

I told her Ralph had bought it for Kate.

'He bought a gift for me?' Her eyes widened and she put down her sewing.

'No, he bartered it. My brother doesn't believe in coin.' I realised I'd said too much and promptly shut my mouth.

'Why?'

I was suddenly defiant, wanted to put her off her lik-ing for Ralph. 'He says that's where the fault lies in the world. It's one of the ideas of the Diggers. That the earth belongs to all men equally, not just to lords and ladies like you.'

Lady Katherine laughed. 'The earth cannot belong to all men equally. What about simpletons, or ne-er-do-wells? These are strange ideas. And does your brother think land-owners like me should be cast out of our houses so that the simpletons can move in?'

How dare she laugh at him! 'I don't know milady.'

'What else does your brother say?'

I shook my head stubbornly, realising I could get him into trouble.

'We will keep the horse, as it was a gift to me. I will try to persuade Mr Grice to let me ride in the grounds. You will accompany me on my rides out, at least until my husband returns.'

In the afternoon I mopped the long gallery, but Mistress Binch called me in the middle of it and the next thing I knew one of Grice's men appeared and grabbed me by the ear. Mr Grice shouted and railed at me. I'd forgotten to move the mop and bucket and he'd tripped over it. Two day's pay would be deducted from my wages to pay for his ruined breeches. Two days of hard work wasted. I rubbed my sore ear and nearly wept.

Later when I came up to draw the curtains against the dark, I saw Mr Grice tell Lady Katherine I was a waste of money.

'I have to have someone,' she said. 'It would be unseemly for me to be alone in a house full of men.'

So I waited until the evening before I dared broach the subject of my day off. 'I know I've not been here a month yet milady, but I was wondering – may I have a day off on Sunday?'

'Why Sunday?' she asked.

'To go to church.'

'You're lying. Tell me the real reason or the answer's no.'

'I promised I'd meet someone.'

'Your brother?'

I shook my head trying to fend off the inevitable.

'Tell me. Then I'll decide.'

I sighed. 'He's going over to Iver to meet the Diggers, he said I could go with him.'

'You can take Sunday off, as it's the Lord's Day.' I was about to thank her, but then she smiled, 'As long as Kate can go with you.'

I curtseyed with my face set like a stone.

The day we were to go to the Diggers proved dry and bright. Mr Grice had said we might walk out round the grounds, and he seemed distracted, told us he was going to St Albans to talk business with an army friend.

We gave his men the slip by going out the back way past the stables. When we set off calves were tottering in the fields, the grass was thick with daisies and the sky full of scudding clouds. This time my mistress changed her clothes in the old tithe barn at the edge of the estate.

'Shall we ride there?' Lady Katherine's face was eager, her hair pulled back under my kitchen coif.

'No,' I said shortly. 'You ride like a lady.'

'And how does a lady ride?'

'Like she owns the highway.'

Lady Katherine seemed to find this amusing, 'Maybe I do,' she said.

I ignored it and gestured at her to hurry, though it made me uncomfortable, this reversal where I was telling her what to do again.

The party of people gathered at the common were a motley bunch, mostly young men, but there were couples with children too. I was glad to see neither my sister Elizabeth, nor John Soper, nor his ill-mannered son were present, but my heart gave a little jump to see Jacob Mallinson. Last time I saw him, I'd been crying and my eyes had been all red. I turned away, embarrassed, pretended I hadn't seen him. To my surprise when I looked back he was walking over.

'Good morrow, Abigail.' Jacob took off his hat and waited expectantly to be introduced. Of course – it was my mistress that drew his eye, not me.

'This is Kate,' I said, helplessly. Something about her poise made her stand out. Jacob would never look at me next to her.

Jacob was naming himself when my brother appeared all in a hurry. He ignored me, and pushed in front of Jacob, turning his full attention to Kate. 'I'm so glad you could come. It's a lovely day, isn't it?'

To give Lady Katherine her due, she did not answer but just dipped her head. A pink tinge had found its way to her cheeks, a pink tinge that was even now showing equally on Ralph's face. Jacob stepped back to give them room.

Ralph handed her up onto the cart and she accepted gracefully and prettily. But then of course she did, she was used to behaving like a lady. A niggle of jealousy wormed in my stomach. I struggled up after her with no help from my brother, but Jacob Mallinson climbed up after me and sat at my side. His presence next to me made me hot and tongue-tied.

The convoy of carts set off along the main track following those on horseback.

'I hear you are working at Markyate Manor now,' Jacob said. 'How do you like it?'

'Well enough.' I guarded my tongue because Lady Katherine could hear.

'It's just they're saying in the village that they're finished, that the Fanshawes have no rightful heir. The land might be sold and come back to the people then.'

Lady Katherine turned, 'No. The Fanshawes will keep their lands.'

Ralph began to talk to her then, quickly and impassioned, trying to convince her of the Diggers' ideals. I caught the gist of most of it. He said that since Parliament had come to power, all lands granted by the King to landlords and priests were illegal, and that the laws set by the Normans – the 'yoke of tyranny' he called it – had been removed. So now the common land should be returned to the common people. 'Like Winstanley says, how can we have a Commonwealth with no wealth in common?' he asked.

As he spoke I could not watch Lady Katherine's face, but when he had finished her face was stony and she turned her head away. She gripped her seat tight and stared out with troubled eyes at the passing landscape.

I felt sorry for her, it must feel horrible to be despised by your tenants. I did not dare reach out to comfort her because I was not sure who I was comforting, the Lady Katherine, or the servant Kate.

Jacob must have caught the atmosphere because he gave me a brief puzzled smile. Even his smile made me feel all bothered.

When we reached the village of Iver, two men – Mr Whistler and Mr Barton – came out to greet us. We left the horses in a clearing with some of their friends whilst they took us to look at the common land where they had built their Digger community and sowed crops.

We stopped at a patch of land which showed less weed than the rest of the common. Lady Katherine stayed close behind me, still quiet. I saw Ralph move in beside her protectively, and Jacob on her other side. I got the feeling that while she was there I could have burst into flames and nobody would have noticed.

'Look, the remains of one of our houses,' Mr Barton said.

I stared at the tumbledown mud and stick walls, at the bare earth floor. It looked like a place only fit for sheep or goats.

'There were five like this, with two families in each, but they came in the night and tore off the roofs and hacked them down with picks and hoes.'

I did not dare look at Lady Katherine. I was ashamed. I don't know what I had imagined, but I knew I didn't want to live like that, in a squalid hovel with no proper floor and no fireplace, everyone all squashed together in the dirt. I could not imagine why Ralph would either.

And Lady Katherine must think us all swine to want to live in such a way. What on earth would she think, coming from her polished oak floors, her tapestry cushions and her fine silks?

'This is where our barley grew,' Mr Barton said, leaning down to pick out one straggling green shoot. 'But they'll not finish us. We're hoping other places will try it and as one place goes down, we'll try somewhere else. Like rabbits, we'll pop up on every bit of common land until there are too many of us for them to deny us our rights.'

I stood uneasily whilst Ralph asked Mr Whistler and Mr Barton many questions and they pointed out the ruins where cottages had been, the fire pits still visible in the turf, the remains of fences where they had kept pigs and mutton. It looked pathetic to me, like a child's attempt to build a town with mud and water.

'They fired the houses, beat our women with sticks to drive them away,' Mr Barton said. 'Even though we were peaceable. I can still hear the women's cries in my head, sometimes. Screams and calling out to merciful God.' He swallowed. 'It is not something you forget.' He paused, rubbed his forehead, 'But we can't do it again here, it took the juice out of us and we just haven't enough men willing.'

I looked to see milady's reaction. 'Who did this? Who burnt your houses?' Lady Katherine's words were clear and sharp.

'The lords of the manors and the Sherriff. To stop us building it back up. They are not content with keeping us off the land they own, but they want to keep us off our common land too, the land that belongs to all of us, the land we fought for against the King.'

Lady Katherine had forgotten who she was supposed to be, she was standing very tall, and she opened her mouth imperiously to speak again. I trod hard down with my heel on her foot. She flinched but closed her mouth. Ralph took her silence for agreement and threw her a sympathetic look.

Ralph and the rest of the men left us then at the clearing with the horses whilst they strode away, talking enthusiastically. They were going to meet with General Winstanley who was the leader of the Digger movement. Winstanley lived close by, lodging with a friend, the gentleman who had taken his family in, after the failure of the last Digger venture.

'Winstanley's given up,' Barton shook his head sadly, 'but perhaps if enough of us show we are still willing, he'll come back alongside us for the cause.'

Lady Katherine and I stayed with the other women. Margery, one of the older ones, had thought to bring bread and cheese wrapped in a cloth, and she offered us a share. We spread out the cloth on the ground to keep our skirts from the dirt.

'Do you think Ralph will persuade Winstanley to help them?' I asked her before I bit into my bread, secretly hoping that she'd say no. I could not imagine a future scrabbling there on the common, worse off than the hunt dogs.

'I doubt it. Winstanley's looking to try another approach. But your brother won't give up, and he'll lead us right enough, he's got the fire in him. We all like Ralph; his heart's in the right place.'

'The only trouble is,' said a younger woman dandling a baby on her lap, 'it needs organising. There's some set dead against us, and it's hard to find a place to meet, one that's not going to rouse up suspicion.'

'You could meet at Markyate Manor.'

I turned to stare at Lady Katherine. She couldn't be serious.

The younger woman laughed, 'That's a good one!'

'No. I mean it. In the old threshing barn,' Lady Katherine said. 'It's empty and nobody goes there. We've just been there, haven't we, Abi?'

Had she taken leave of her senses?

'But what about the Fanshawes and their servants?' asked Margery, pausing in cutting the cheese, 'It would be trespass and treason if they caught us.'

'It's a cock-eyed idea,' I said.

'No,' the young woman said. 'Kate's right. It's the last place they'd think we'd meet. If there's really an empty barn there, I say, we put it to Ralph, see what he says.'

'He'll say no,' I sulked.

Margery said, 'They say young Lady Katherine's gone stark mad anyway. Is it true? Henshaw, the servant who came from there, says Lady Katherine ripped all the paintings off the walls and the drapes from the windows and wanders about in only her shift.'

Kate was so taken aback that she could not speak.

I could not resist. 'It's all true, every word,' I said. 'There's only three of us servants there now, and the stable boys will only come in the daylight hours because they're frightened of what Lady Katherine might do at night –'

My mistress had recovered; she looked at me archly. 'Yes. We have to lock our doors, and sometimes after dark we can hear her growling and scrabbling to get in –
'

The young woman's eyes had grown round and wide, 'Lord have mercy!'

Lady Katherine realised she was on the edge of going too far. 'Anyway, she wouldn't notice if we were to meet in the barn. It's far from the house. The only person to watch out for is my...the manservant Mr Grice. Nothing gets past him and his servants. But he can't walk far because of his bad foot. And there are no other staff.'

We ate then, and I worried about whether Ralph would agree to them meeting at Markyate Manor. I fidgeted, restless, my legs wanting to run away from the dilemma. If I told Ralph who Kate really was then she would certainly dismiss me and I would have lost the only job I ever had. If I didn't tell him, then he'd want to meet at the Manor right under the noses of the gentry he was so set against.

When the men returned from Winstanley they were subdued.

'Well?' Margery waited for Ralph to speak.

'He gave us his blessing,' Jacob said, 'but he won't join us.'

I could see Ralph's disappointment in the set of his head and shoulders.

'But good news, Ralph. Kate here has found us a place to meet.' The young woman smiled at Kate. 'We'll not be giving up, will we? My Will didn't lose his life fighting the King for nothing, did he?'

'No, Susan, he did not.' Ralph braced his shoulders, stuck out his chin. 'We'll not let it discourage us, we'll go ahead all the same. Maybe Winstanley will change his mind when he sees how our community grows and thrives. And now Kate's found us a meeting place.' He gave her a dazzling smile. 'It must be a good omen!' He began to sing,

'The poor long
Have suffered wrong,
By the gentry of this nation,'

I loved to watch singing, to see the words stretched into shapes like skins. Soon the rest of the party were joining in the song, swaying together, arms about each other's shoulders, except Jacob who looked mighty uncomfortable. Like me, he probably couldn't sing a note. Lady Katherine was looking at the ground uncertain what to do, but Ralph lay his arm across her shoulder and soon she and I were enfolded into the group as they sang;

...And then we shall see
Brave community,
When valleys lie level with mountains.

When they'd done, there was a cheer of jubilation and shaking of fists. Ralph let go and Kate looked modestly down at her feet.

I despaired. I did not know how to stop my brother, how to tell him that he and his friends the Diggers were playing right into Royalist hands.

I could not speak to Lady Katherine all the way back. When we arrived at the barn the sun was low in the sky.

'We'd best be quick. Mr Grice might be back from inspecting the farms and he won't like us being out after dusk.' Kate was already down to her shift, and thrusting my skirts into a bag.

After a moment I could stand it no more and asked, 'Why? Why do you want the Diggers meeting on your land? What will you do to them?'

'Do to them?' She paused, puzzled, with her bodice in her hands.

'Yes. I know you will wait until they are gathered and then send Mr Grice or your menfolk after them.'

'No. You're wrong. You don't understand.' She leaned towards me, serious. 'I want them here. I know how it feels to be dispossessed. I know what it feels like to be beaten for no real reason.'

'But what about your husband, and Mr Grice?'

'I hate them all.' Her eyes lit up with a dark intensity. 'You don't know how good it feels to pull the wool over their eyes. I love the idea that the very people they want to fight are plotting right here. They call it their land, but really it is mine – from my mother's estate. And I shall have on it whom I choose. Besides, do you think I have no heart? I can see your brother is a fine man, and the Diggers are good people who only want to live in peace.'

She turned for me to lace her up. When it was done I asked, 'Will you tell them then, who you are?' I was hopeful.

'No.' She shrugged her shoulders at me. 'I like being Kate. I don't want to go back to being Lady Katherine. They'll hate me. As long as you keep quiet, nobody need know.'

'No. Please don't ask me to. I can't. I can't lie to Ralph like that.'

'You will do as I ask.' The proud Lady Katherine was back.

I bridled under her command, fear for my brother making me instantly mutinous. 'I'm not taking orders. Not with you dressed in my kitchen coif.'

Her hand flew to her head. I saw the annoyance flit over her face. She pulled off the cap and placed it deliberately on the hay bale between us. It was a challenge and I took it.

'If you make me lie to Ralph, I'll find another position,' I said.

She looked up at me with calculating green eyes. 'Not without a reference, you won't.'

CHAPTER NINE

Gloves and Mud

Since Sir Simon and Sir Thomas had gone, I was allowed back to sleep in my own room. That night I lay in my bed in the flickering candlelight, and tussled the dilemma in my mind. I could not believe I'd dared to talk back to my mistress the way I had. It was because of her being dressed as a servant. It had me all confused.

But what if I left and got no recommendation from Lady Katherine? Then the chances of me working again were slim, even if I wasn't deaf. Everyone set great store by their reference papers and to have none marked you out as a lazy or dishonest worker. I realised that a spat with Lady Katherine could affect my prospects for life – an uneasy thought. I would just have to buckle down and keep my place here, there was no other way.

I turned over, but I still could not sleep. I stood and went to the window where a pale moon flitted between the clouds. I would have to do as my mistress said and go along with it – let the Diggers meet here at the Manor and say nothing about who Kate really was.

A movement near the trees caught my attention. A glint of metal, a flash of something white. I peered out but the moon disappeared behind the clouds. I was just beginning to think I'd imagined it and was about to turn away when the moon sailed out from the clouds and I saw a man leading her ladyship's horse past the house. I was sure it was her horse because of his white blaze. The man was cowled and had a dark hat pulled low on the forehead. I watched them pass, and something about the man's furtive manner, the way he glanced to right and left, made me think he shouldn't be there – perhaps it was one Grice's men, or one of the stable-lads. What a cheek, riding out on her ladyship's horse without her knowledge.

The next day I asked her about it. 'Beg your pardon, but I saw a man riding out on Blaze last night, very late. I thought I should tell you, Milady.'

Her eyes opened very wide, before she said decisively, 'No. You must be imagining it.'

'I saw it, clear as anything. It was a bright moon and I –'

'You're mistaken. There's an end of it.'

But I knew what I had seen, and something about her reaction bothered me.

It was not the first time I had noticed something, and Lady Katherine had told me I was wrong. The first time was when I found my mistress's glove lying on the grass by the stable as I went to fetch water from the well. I noticed it because I had definitely folded both her gloves away in her trunk myself, only the night before. I picked it up, puzzled, and examined it. It was still early and Lady Katherine was slow to waken that morning, despite me bringing her a jug of cold water to wash with.

'Look, I just found your glove,' I said, holding it up before her face, 'over by the stable. I wonder how it got there.'

'I don't know,' she said, sleepily, 'I must've dropped it yesterday.'

'But I put it away last night. Have you got two pairs?'

'No.' Now she sat up, awake, watching me. 'You must have forgotten, I don't know how it got there.'

I sensed something wary in her attitude, and the way she stared at my face. And she looked tired, there were dark circles under her eyes.

A few days later I found the brooch lying under her mirror on her dressing table. It was the one Lady Ann had been wearing when she came to dinner. I'd noticed the brooch particularly because it was shaped like a thistle with a large purple stone set in it, and I remembered thinking the stone was so large it could not possibly be real.

'Lady Ann has left her brooch,' I said.

'No. It's mine,' Lady Katherine said, plucking it up quickly from where it lay.

'But Lady Ann had one just like it —'

'You're mistaken,' she said.

'Yes milady,' I said, knowing I wasn't. 'Are you going to wear it?'

'No,' she said sharply, 'not today.' And she pushed it away to the bottom of the marquetry box where she kept her trinkets.

I remember thinking it was strange. So that was the second thing.

They say things run in threes, and I didn't have to wait long for the third.

When I woke the next day it was a beautiful day, but unseasonably hot and airless. There had been a welcome downpour in the night and now the sun was making the fields steam. I thought I would open the windows and doors to let a little air through, so I went into Thomas's adjoining room to throw open the windows. As I walked across I saw that his lordship's tallboy was open and I went over to shut it. His black wool cloak was dangling there from a hook, but the hem was damp and full of mud.

I hesitated. It needed to dry out and be brushed. I pulled it out and lay it out on the chair, puzzling over it. As I did so, a pair of his breeches tumbled out and a shirt. All were damp. I put my nose to them, but they smelt fresh, not like a dampness that had been there for weeks. A faint scent tugged at my senses – cinnamon and rose, like the Lady Katherine, but it was so faint I did not know if it came from the cloak or my memory.

As far as I knew, the men had not returned. So who had worn these? Pushed to the back of the shelf were a pair of Thomas's boots, the mud still wet on the soles. I left them alone, but went downstairs to ask Mistress Binch if the men had been back.

'No. I wish they would. It's hardly worth cooking anything elaborate for just one. Lady Katherine and Mr Grice have to make do with servant fare when they are away, and it's so dull making it.'

I did not tell her why I asked.

A few days later Lady Katherine asked me if I would clean his lordship's riding clothes. 'He will be home soon, and he must have forgotten to ask you. When they are done, you can put them away in his closet. And leave me the brushes, in case I should need to do my own shoes.'

'But I'll do them for you milady, you only need to ask –'

'I would like to do them myself occasionally,' she said. 'It will amuse me, help me to feel more like a serving maid.'

'Very good milady.'

I was not taken in. My mistress certainly knew about the dirty riding clothes or she would not have asked me to clean them. Who took her horse at night? The stable boys? Was Lady Katherine allowing someone else to borrow her husband's clothes?

And now I had seen the evidence with my own eyes – someone was taking Blaze out at night, but it was someone Lady Katherine knew all about. Then why was I not to know? She made me feel stupid though I knew I wasn't. I could not make sense of it, and in the end I ceased to try. My mother's words came back to me – 'a good servant must keep quiet and ask no questions'.

And I had enough problems. Lady Katherine wanted to be Kate whenever a Digger's meeting was called, and we had to get to the barn early and leave late so I could help her dress. It irked me every time, though I tried not to show it and to be a good servant. This was the fifth meeting they had had at the barn in as many weeks and every time my heart was in my mouth in case Mr Grice or his servants might catch us in the barn instead of strolling in the grounds, or in case any of the Diggers arrived early.

The weather had turned warm and dry, so one of the double doors swung a little ajar to allow a breeze. Ralph had rallied support amongst his friends so the barn now held about fifteen people, mostly young men, but some women too, all animatedly discussing the plans for the new Digger community on Nomansland Common.

'I hope we get more rain soon,' Jacob said, 'or the planting will be hard. We'll stand or fall by this first harvest.'

'What do you think, Abi? Can you feel anything?' Ralph mimed rain and raised his eyebrows questioningly. He always asked me because I was good at sensing changes in the air.

'No rain yet. The air's still as pond water,' I said.

But despite this, I was restless, the straw bale I was sitting on prickled through my skirts. I was also spitting mad because Lady Katherine had made me sew a new coarse wool skirt and sleeves, and I had worked hard on them all week before realising they were for her, not for me. So there she sat in her new skirt and sleeves, drawing all the young men's eyes and most especially the eyes of my brother.

I looked at her now and the sight of her made me even more enraged. The fact she spoke little seemed to make her more alluring. Last week Ralph had said she was delightful - so shy and modest, just the way a maid should be. I felt like slapping him, and had to go away and howl my frustration by kicking at the stone gatepost. Wouldn't you know, Jacob Mallinson saw me doing it, and he looked at me as though I had lost my reason.

At the meeting there was talk of building four houses on the common, and everyone was assigned tasks or certain labours to do. I said I'd gather wood for the fires, and I was astonished when Kate volunteered she would go with them to set up the kitchen by building a hearth and arranging a trestle for the pot. I simply could not imagine it, milady doing such work.

'Your mistress seems very lax with her servants. That's the third time in a month you have both had a half-day,' Jacob said to me, and rubbed his neck, perplexed.

'She is ill abed, and cares not what we do,' Kate said, before I could answer.

'But I heard she's a hard taskmaster, isn't that right, Abi? She made Abi scrub all the windows for hours last week until her hands were sore,' Ralph said.

A blush spread up Kate's neck. 'Our mistress does not mean to be so harsh, I'm sure.'

'Never fear Kate, soon you'll have no masters but the wind and weather,' Ralph said.

'Here's to that day!' Jacob slapped him on the back.

I looked at Jacob in his neat breeches and white shirt. I could not imagine him living in a cob-built shelter. He had grown up in a fine brick house with his father, the elected constable of the village, and now he had a tithe cottage on the Fanshawe estate. He did not seem to fit into this rough labourer's life. I couldn't help but wonder if Jacob's father knew of his son's plans.

It was agreed by all that we would go to the common at first light, and quietly, so that we would have order established before anyone at the village could prevent us.

Dusk had fallen during our talking and I opened the door wider to catch some moonlight so as to see better what folk were saying. We were just finishing our business when I caught a wisp of movement near the door. Someone was listening. I jumped up and hurried to the door, and was just in time to see the white apron tails of Mistress Binch whisk around the side of the barn. I sprinted after her but she was quick as a hare and soon in behind the kitchen door.

Fortunately we had all had our backs to her. What if she'd seen Lady Katherine? If she had, she might tell Sir Simon, and I'd be certain to be blamed for giving her my clothes. A knot of fear rolled in my stomach.

I tugged at Kate's sleeve, 'Please milady –'

Kate frowned, 'Sssh!' She was listening to a woman called Susan who was addressing the women.

'Sorry. Mistress Binch was listening behind the door.'

'What?' Kate's eyebrows shot up in alarm. 'Did she see me?'

'I don't think so, but –'

'What's the matter?' Ralph appeared.

'The cook was spying on us,' I said. 'I don't know how much she heard, but enough I'd say, enough to guess your purpose.'

He frowned. 'Curses. Is she for us or against us?'

'I don't know, but she'll likely tell Mr Grice, the overseer.'

'What about Lady Katherine? Will she tell her?'

'I doubt it,' I said, 'Mistress Binch hardly ever goes near her. She ...well, she sends me to take messages if she needs to speak to her.'

'It's a blow. We hoped to keep it quiet until we had the houses up and smoke coming from the chimneys. They can't stop us once the smoke's rising, it's an ancient bylaw. But it's too late to do anything now. We'd better get away from here.'

Ralph took Kate by the arm. They were in the shadow now, away from our lanterns. He whispered in her ear and they both laughed. Her expression was confiding, intimate. Then he lifted her hand to his lips and kissed it, before following the others who were hastening out of the door.

I turned away, a cold feeling spreading across my chest. Kate watched him go, like a love-struck fool.

When Jacob Mallinson caught me by the elbow I was distracted - angry with Kate and Ralph for shutting me out. Jacob said something, but it had got too dark to catch his words. Frustrated and bewildered by not being able to make out he was saying, I just shook my head.

He looked a bit affronted, gave a curt nod and then ran to catch up with the others. Afterwards I realised with shame that he had been offering to walk me back to the house. This often happened; that I'd puzzle over something someone said and the key in my mind would turn too late.

Curses. My stomach contracted with longing. Jacob Mallinson, none other than the constable's son, had wanted to walk with me. Me, Abigail Chaplin. I groaned in frustration and wished I could have that moment back. Yes, I would have said to Jacob. Yes please.

I winced, put my hands to my hot cheeks. I had been rude and unmannerly. No wonder no young man would look twice at me. It wasn't because I was deaf, it was because I was foolish and ill-mannered. Ashamed of myself, I followed my mistress back towards the lights of the house. Later, I was distracted when Lady Katherine needed to be dressed, and I could not say a word.

'Ralph kissed my hand!' she said, raising the back of it to her lips.

I tugged her hair hard with the hairbrush.

'Careful!' she turned and shot a look at me, as if to say, 'what do you think you're doing?'

I curbed my temper. Above all, I needed to keep my place.

CHAPTER TEN

Demands and Promises

The next morning I was to air all the bedroom drapes. I had taken them from the beds and strung up on the line. I watched them sway in the breeze, thinking about the mystery of Lady Katherine's gloves and the wet clothes in the closet, and about how my mistress seemed to be sweet on Ralph.

I was about to hang another bundle when I saw a man approaching down the drive on foot. Something about the way he walked was familiar. It looked like my father. But it couldn't be. My father was dead. It must be a travelling tinker. I batted at the drapes half-heartedly, and the dust rose up in clouds, but still I peered through it, my eyes fixed on the lone figure on the drive.

It couldn't be Father because the captain had brought us word that all his platoon were lost and Mother had wept for weeks. But a great wave was rising in my chest, and before I knew it I was running, a shout of 'Father!' behind my lips but unable to come.

He saw me and began to run too. A few yards away, he stopped, his eyebrows shooting up under the brim of his hat. 'My, you're all grown up,' he said, before I bumped into his chest and threw my arms about him. He smelt of gunpowder and leather, and the tobacco he always smoked in his clay pipe.

He pushed me gently away. 'There, there,' he said. 'Stand away so I can see you.'

I stood back, shyly, tears wet on my face.

'What a beautiful young woman. Where did my little mouse Abigail go? A lady's maid, no less, so Mother tells me.'

So he had already been home. 'What happened?' I asked, when we had embraced a long while, 'Where've you been?'

'I was captured and held hostage by the King's Army. Until some of the kind folk of Berwick raised money to buy our freedom. We had to promise to change sides and fight for the King, but once free we scattered and found our way home, and the King can find another bunch of turncoats to do his dirty business. But I'm looking for Ralph, we need him. Him and any other men we can muster.'

'He's not here.'

'Do you know where he is?'

I shook my head mutely. But I did know. He was with the Diggers, gone to lay foundations for the houses on the Common, though instinct told me he would not want my father there. Father always put a dampener on what he called 'Ralph's foolish ideas'.

'Can I come home now Father?'

'Why? You have a position here don't you? Mother told me how glad she was that you had work at last. It's hard for her with Martha and William still so young.'

'I thought that since you were back –'

'I'll be away again soon. There's a big push at Wigan in the North, and then the army is headed south, probably to Worcester. The King's bound to go there – it's his last hope, the only Royalist stronghold left. We need more fighting men to finish them. Ralph can come with me.'

'No Father, please. Don't go. Not again.'

'I have to.'

'But you've only just come back.' I clung to his buff jerkin like I had when I was a child. 'And what about Mother? How will she manage without you and Ralph?'

'General Fleetwood has a plan to bridge the river Severn with pontoons, because the King will only fortify the East side of the city, thinking we can't cross. Ralph is good with these tasks, knows about river flow. We need him. He will come with me, to meet up with the rest of the New Model Army in Wigan, before we march South again.'

I began to protest again. Father hadn't seen our long hours of waiting for news of him, his casual decision to be off to the wars again made me want to strike him. He pressed his hand on the top of my head as if he understood.

I looked up in time to see him say, 'Your mother will manage. It's good you and Elizabeth are working. You're grown enough now to stand on your own two feet. And your mother will find someone else to help in the fields. The women will pull together as they always have. And don't worry, I will take care of Ralph, bring him home safe.'

I stared down at the parched ground. Bitter disappointment made tears threaten. I had hoped he would take me home, back to my familiar cottage, back to my family. I didn't want to live in the big house with its gloomy chambers, but nor did I want to live in some scraped-together pigsty with Ralph. But at the same time I knew I was too old now to be living at home with Mother; that I should be looking for a young man to build a future with. But who would want a deaf girl like me?

Father was still talking about his plans for defeating the King. But I could not believe Ralph would want to go with him, full of fire for the Diggers as he was. But Father might persuade him. Ralph would be soft, seeing as Father was only just returned to us, and had already gone through so much for Parliament's cause.

'Abigail, I have to do what's right.' My father was gentle now, his eyes tender. Though he was back, I could not forget the feeling of when he was lost, and I clung tight to his arm.

'When the war is won, we will have the power to govern ourselves – Cromwell will ensure a right government.' He smiled, though his eyes were sad. 'I have to go. I wish it was otherwise, but bear up. You are old enough to make your own life.' I wiped my eyes with my sleeve as he talked. 'One thing though – make sure to see your mother when you can. She misses you and worries.'

'Yes Father.'

'That's better. Now where is my Ralph? Have you seen him?'

I shook my head again.

'I will try Elizabeth at the apothecary's then. And I look forward to the end of all this toil. The King's rallied an army of Scots against us, but they're untrained, just a rabble with no proper plans. We're confident we can finish them if we can gather enough men. But say nothing of this to the Fanshawes, you understand?'

'Yes, I understand.'

'And if you hear anything from them of the Royalist plans – anything at all, you must tell me, or get word to the landlord at the Green Man.'

I nodded.

'Promise?'

I promised, though it was with a heavy heart. I was to be everyone's eyes it seemed. When my father left I felt as though I was a rag, wrung dry. It was almost as if I had imagined him – we had been nine months without him and the wound of his absence was so nearly healed. Now I might have to lose him all over again, but not only him, Ralph too.

At the house I hoped nobody had seen us talking. I told Mistress Binch I had been on an errand for Lady Katherine, and Lady Katherine that I had been on an errand for Mistress Binch, for I could not tell either of them that my father was back and plotting the King's downfall. I was watching my step all the time now, as if balancing on a knife blade. Everyone seemed to have so many secrets. Why could people not be straightforward? One slip and I would be done for.

I felt bad about the letters too. Mail had come for Lady Katherine from her husband, but I did not dare disobey Mr Grice, though I suspected they never got from him to my mistress. And Lady Katherine wrote to her husband – thin dutiful letters, but again these went to Mr Grice. I told myself I was simply obeying orders, that it was none of my business, but my conscience prickled just the same.

As for Grice, he spent most of his time in the reading room now at the front of the house poring over the household accounts. It was fortunate - because if he'd seen my father hanging about, it would have caused a stink, of that I was certain.

When it was time to prepare Lady Katherine for bed she told me I must sleep in her room again from now on. I sighed, for I had been in my own chamber whilst the men were away, and it was at least a place where I could be at peace with my thoughts, out of the scrutiny of my employers.

But Lady Katherine was insistent. 'Royalists are on their way with more troops to aid the King. A messenger came yesterday to tell Grice and I overheard them. I'm nervous, I never know when they might come.'

'But Mistress Binch says the King is in Scotland, gathering troops there.'

'Yes, but the news is, he is bringing them south and they will try to destroy the Roundhead strongholds in Luton and St Albans.' She paused in combing her hair. 'Last time, troops were garrisoned here. They scare me, all these men with blood on their hands.'

My father's face came back to me, his words that I should tell him if I heard any information. I wondered if I could pretend not to have understood what she said.

Lady Katherine went on, 'I hate all this bloodshed. I wish I could live the life your brother describes, the Diggers life - one of peace and harmony with the earth.'

'It's a hard life, milady. Not what you think. It would not suit a lady who is not used to it.'

She put down her comb. 'Your brother has a lot of followers for his ideas. He must be admired by many young women.'

'I suppose so.'

'Has he made promises to anyone yet?'

I gave her a sharp look. 'He hasn't the time. I expect it will come soon enough.' I was unwilling to tell her more. After all, she was married already, it was none of her business.

'I wonder what he is doing right now...' Her eyes drifted to the window.

I cut in on her thoughts. 'Digging on the common, as long as there's light enough. Raising foundations or turning over the land. He won't waste daylight if he can use it for producing crops. Many folk have never forgotten the bad years, those three years of failed harvests and famine.'

She turned at my voice. 'That would be before I was married.'

'Yes milady, dark years. Years I don't want to think about.'

She stood and turned back the bedcovers, and I hurried to help. She took hold of my arm to get my attention. 'So why does Ralph want to farm the common so badly if he already farms land of his own?'

I marvelled that she could be so stupid. 'It is your land, milady. He is just a tenant farmer. What we harvest is little enough, but the bulk of it comes to you as tithes. He wants to be his own man.' I pulled away from her. I did not want to mention my father.

I saw her take this in. 'Your family are my tenants?'

'Yes milady. My mother and my young brother and sister. They rely on Ralph to tend the crops, and now he's got this puddle-headed idea of digging up the common. I don't know how they'll manage.' I pushed away the image of my father and his words; that he would take Ralph to war.

Her eyebrows knitted together in a frown as she saw my worried face. 'People will help them, I'm sure.'

'I expect so, milady, but he can't be in two places at once. The harvesting is hard work, but then so is digging foundations for houses.'

'I will help with the digging, I have already told Ralph I will.'

I stared at her.

'Ralph seems to think I could do it,' her eyes took on a defiant glint.

I could not stop the words bursting out, 'But that's because he doesn't know who you are! He thinks you're Kate! That you're used to hard work, to carrying heavy coals, to chopping firewood. There'll be nobody to make your fires or wash your clothes on the common. You saw those houses – they're like kennels. You can't tell me you want to live there, it's scraping a living from the sweat of your own hands.'

Lady Katherine shrugged. 'I could do that. It can't be that difficult. I'm thinking I'll join the Diggers and live

their way. I like them. It's the first time I've been welcome anywhere.' She tied back her hair in a ribbon, un-
concerned.

I swear my mouth fell open. 'But what about your
husband? What about this house?'

'Him? I care not a jot for him. And my greedy stepfather will sell the house from under me to pay the
King's debts. The Diggers accepted me. Ralph said they
take anyone who believes in their cause.'

'They would not welcome you if they knew you were
Lady Katherine Fanshawe whose family fleeces them
dry each year for their rents, whose kinfolk slaughtered
theirs in the last battle at Gloucester.'

'Enough.' Her eyes took on a hue of steel.

Horrified, I realised I'd gone too far.

'I don't know why I am arguing with a servant,' she
said icily. 'Nobody needs to know who I am. You will
do as I say. You will continue to accompany me to the
meetings in the barn.'

'In the Digger community, there are no servants. We
are all equal. You cannot have it both ways. If you are a
Digger then we are equals.'

There was a moment's stunned pause, whilst I marvelled at my own boldness and she scrutinized me to see
if I would back down. I stood my ground.

'You will take me to the Common to help Ralph and
the others or your family will be cease to be my tenants.'

I was silent then. My mother's face floated before my eyes. Had I not caused her enough trouble, but I must bring her more?

My anger turned inwards to make me stiff and cold. I tucked down my mistress's sheets with deliberate movements, held up the corner as she climbed in with my face turned away from her. She did not speak, and if she had I would have pretended not to understand.

The next day I took Pepper and rode out before anyone was awake to tell Ralph his father was home. He was shocked, and at first could not take it in, but set off immediately to see for himself. During the day Lady Katherine and I kept up the pretence of mistress and maid, uncertain how else to behave with each other. It gave me an ache in the chest, this bad feeling between us.

But that evening the Diggers met at Jacob Mallinson's orchard. I refused to take orders from Kate in her homespun and apron, and besides I could bear the atmosphere no longer. So when she sat next to me on the cloth that was spread on the ground, I got up and moved away.

Ralph went over to speak with Kate and sat down next to her. A few minutes later he beckoned me over but I shook my head.

Finally he came over. 'What's the matter?'

'Nothing.'

Ralph looked uncomfortable. 'I went to see Father. I could not believe it, him turning up after all this time. He said he was proud of you, working at last,' he said.

'I can't believe he was here. It seems like a dream.'

'He seemed different from how I remembered. Smaller somehow. I can't believe he'd do that to Mother, just appear from nowhere and then abandon her all over again. I told him so, and I got a bit heated, and well... we had an argument.'

'Oh Ralph. You and your temper. It will blow over.' I made a sign of wind blowing over my palm.

'No.' He twisted his hat in his hands. 'He's told me not to go back home, that I'm not welcome there.'

'No. That can't be true. Why? What happened?'

He signed, 'He wanted me to join him and fight for Parliament, but I refused. I want to try our way, the new way of the Diggers. Since he went away I've become my own man, I'm seventeen, I don't want to be told what to do any more, like a little boy.'

'But what about Mother?'

'She sides with him. She says I must have respect and obey father if I'm to stay under his roof. Anyway, it's too late now. I was just telling Kate, the Diggers plans have advanced, because I'll be needing somewhere to live. We're going for the day after tomorrow. Market day. Folks will be busy and we'll get a bit of a start. You'll be there, won't you? Kate says she will.'

'I wouldn't rely on Kate.'

'What's the matter? Have you fallen out with each other?'

I made a face.

'It will blow over.'

'That's what I said about you and Father. But you're wrong, it won't. Kate's not what you think.'

'What have you got against her all of a sudden? I really like her. She's quiet and comely, and always thinks of others first. Look how she offered to get the hearth and the kitchen built.'

'You don't know her like I do.'

'I think I'm a sound judge of character. And I was glad you two got on so well because I was hoping –'

I turned my head away. I did not want to hear any more. It was my worst nightmare. I knew what he was going to say, that he hoped he might walk out with Kate. And what would happen when he found out he'd set his cap at Lady Katherine Fanshawe?

At that moment Kate stood and came over, 'Would you like some cider? Jacob's brought out a flagon.' She held a cup out to each of us.

I stalked away and went and leant against a tree. When I looked back they were sitting side by side on the cloth, and Kate's eyes kept flicking over to me. Ralph was gazing at her with the look of a man who cannot bear to tear his eyes away. I scowled at them, only to see Jacob Mallinson watching me, his eyebrows furrowed in concern. I groaned inwardly. He would surely think me bad-tempered, when it was none of my fault. Curse my mistress, I wish I'd never set eyes on her.

CHAPTER ELEVEN

Sticks and Stones

A few days later I rushed my duties and went to visit Mother. I was grateful for the summer nights, which meant I could go out later. Since Ralph had told me of his falling out with Father, I wanted to see what Mother thought of it all.

When I arrived she was feeding William with some potage. He was on her knee and she was pushing the food into his mouth with the horn spoon. William looked sickly as usual. He'd never been a strong baby and was always ailing for something. Martha was knitting by the hearth and barely looked up to greet me, she was absorbed in the task as only a six year old can be, with her tongue sticking out of the corner of her mouth.

When I asked her about Ralph she said, 'It will be harder for me with him away. I'll miss him.'

I realised she had already accepted his departure. 'Perhaps he won't go,' I said.

'He must do his duty. But it will mean I must pay for someone to get in the harvest if I want it done. And it has to be done. Unless I give the Fanshawes their portion, they can put me out and get a better tenant.'

'They wouldn't do that.'

She shook her head. 'They put out old Seth Armstrong when he couldn't till the land any more. Don't you remember? Their man, Grice, came and put his furniture out on the step. He had to go to his son. It was so sad. He'd been here twenty years.'

'It won't come to that,' I said, 'I'll make sure it doesn't.' I didn't know how, but I knew my mother was not going to be left without a roof over her head again. I dare not tell her anything about Lady Katherine and Ralph.

'How are you getting along with Lady Katherine?'

I jumped. She must have read my thoughts.

'Well enough,' I said.

Mother frowned and said, 'Are you sure?'

I nodded. I could not trust myself to speak. She drew me over to her arms, and embraced me, but I pushed her away, angry at having to keep so much bottled inside. Soon after, I made my excuses to leave. I saw in her eyes I'd made her sad, but I couldn't help it. Everything seemed to be going wrong.

When I got home I tussled it all in my mind. No use to ask Ralph to be sensible, to forget about the Diggers and help mother with the harvest. Not now he was sweet on my mistress. But now there was my mother and father leaning on him to join the army too. What would he choose? The Diggers were bad enough, but they were harmless. I wanted to slap him, tell him to stay away from Father and Cromwell's men. If he followed Father to the wars, he might get himself killed.

The next day Lady Katherine gave Mistress Binch the day off, because Mr Grice and his men were going out to meet somebody called Wentworth, and would be out all day. Mr Grice had given my mistress some Bible tracts to copy, but I knew his absence meant my mistress would be insistent on us going to the Common.

The day before, I'd come across Grice in the study, surrounded by more deeds and papers. I remembered him forging Sir Simon's name and it made me uneasy. Should I tell my mistress? We were awkward and distant with each other now and it was hard to talk.

When I got to the stable yard Pepper was saddled up along with Blaze, Lady Katherine's finer-boned horse. A stable boy offered to help her up, but Lady Katherine ignored him and swung up into the saddle easily. She was dressed in her green riding habit, but I guessed what was in the carpet bag she carried on her arm. She slung this onto the pommel and we set off. What would happen? Would Kate decide to stay there with the Diggers? I couldn't imagine it. Perhaps her enthusiasm for them was all talk. I worried about my position at the Manor.

Without Lady Katherine, Grice would sack me in an instant.

The weather was warm and sultry. Dark purple clouds hung in the sky. Out of sight of the house Lady Katherine changed into the maid's skirts and thrust her cloak and other clothes under a hedge. Once Lady Katherine was gone, and Kate was in her place she kept trying to catch my eye to speak to me but I would not give her chance.

On the bridleway she hung back so I had to go first and show the way, but as soon as we arrived, a crowd gathered around us to look at Kate's horse.

'Where did you get him?' Jacob asked.

I waited with satisfaction at her discomfort. 'He belongs to Lady Katherine,' Kate said, 'But she doesn't go out any more, so she'll never know.'

'You mean you just took him without asking?' Jacob's face was full of doubt.

Kate patted Blaze on the neck. 'I couldn't bear to see him cooped up every day in the stable. He needed the exercise, poor lad.'

'I suppose you're right. It's a shame to think of an animal like that lying idle,' Jacob agreed. 'Lady Katherine should be glad he's having a run out. Though I can understand you being afraid to ask her; Abigail says she's wild as a cat.'

I did not dare look at her.

Jacob took the horses away to tether them with the others, calling, 'In that central clearing – that's where we'll need the fire.'

I looked around but could not see Ralph. Keen to impress Jacob, I searched around for some stones and lugged the first two and laid them down, before Kate realised what I was doing and came to help. It amused me to see her pick up the rocks and put them next to mine as if they were eggs she was lifting from a nest. They were heavy though and she was soon panting, sweat darkening under the sleeves of her bodice. When we had enough stones I started to dig a pit, but then an idea struck me and I handed Kate the spade. 'You wanted to be a digger. Well, the fire pit needs digging.' Ralph would soon see she would be hopeless in their community.

'How deep?' She picked up the spade and tried to jam it into the earth but it rebounded. We'd had so little rain in the last month.

'Two handspans, maybe.'

I went to gather kindling and when I came back I saw that she was struggling to make an impression on the dry stony soil. I watched her rub her back and then press down with her foot on the top of the blade to try to force it down. Her boots were scuffed and dusty. I smiled to myself and went back to the copse for more wood.

When I got back it was to see Ralph and Jacob digging the pit and Kate standing to one side admiringly.

Furious, I dropped the wood down and said to her, 'if you've nothing to do, go and fetch more wood.'

'All right,' she said, and with a sideways look at Ralph and Jacob she hurried away.

Ralph drew me to one side and rounded on me, his eyes ablaze, 'Who do you think you are, doing the easy work and leaving poor Kate struggling all by herself? We're all in this together and a bit of courtesy to your fellow Diggers costs nothing. Our community stands by our good will to one another. If you can't be peaceable with Kate, then you need to think whether you want to be here at all.'

'But she – '

'I'm seeing another side to you, Abigail, and it's not one I like. Jealousy makes people ugly. Now finish the hearth and for heaven's sake try to treat everyone fair.' He glared at me and strode off.

The injustice of it burned in my chest. Jacob stood up from digging and walked away without even looking at me. The thought that he must think ill of me made me want to cry. But I wouldn't let anyone see. I thumped the rocks down around the pit, ignored Kate when she came to help. But I had to admit, she did try, she heaved boulders and split wood, and by the end of it her hands were just as filthy as mine.

Kate tapped me on the shoulder to get my attention. 'I'm sorry,' she said. 'I saw you arguing with Ralph. I didn't ask them to help,' she said, squatting next to me as we built up the fire, 'he just took the spade out of my hands.'

'You are deceiving him.' I was almost in tears, 'I don't like to see you do that to someone I care for.'

'What makes you think I don't care for him?'

I searched her face and a red flush bloomed on her cheeks in response. I threw down the last sticks. That was all I needed, I saw then that I was too late to stop it, that they were drawn to each other despite the fact they were oil and water, never destined to mix.

Jacob was watching us, so I braced my shoulders and began to shred dry tinder for the fire. The men had built up the dwelling places with wattle and daub and thatched the roofs with bracken before we had the cauldron on the fire to make a stew, but in the distance a forked flash lit up the sky and the first big drops of rain began to fall. I could feel the tingling sensation that always came before a storm. We ignored it, and Kate stirred the pot.

A flicker of white cloth in the trees. I stopped what I was doing to look. A crowd of men was approaching, two on horseback, more on foot. They carried scythes and halberds. My spine prickled.

'Ralph!' I called, 'Jacob!'

Our men came to the clearing and waited as the delegation approached. I recognised John Soper and his loathsome son Ned, Francis Quill the taverner, and a few others. They already had the look of men about to fight, their chins thrust forward, hands gripped into fists or round their weapons.

'Cover your face,' I hissed to Kate, seeing her standing like a mooncalf. She pulled her shawl over her head and mouth.

Jacob took hold of my arm.

'What?' I said.

'Get back to the highway. Quick. We'll meet you at the crossroads.'

'I'm not leaving,' Kate said, 'I'll not be chased away by a few farmers.'

Jacob ignored her. 'You'll be safer. We'll fetch you back later. Now go.' He hauled me by the sleeve and gave me a shove in the direction of the road. I glanced over my shoulder to see that the crowd of men had surrounded our little band of brothers. An angry conversation was in progress and the men pranced on their feet as if waiting for something to begin.

With sickening clarity I saw the moment when Ralph launched his fist at John Soper and the red spurt of blood as it connected, and the two groups blundered into one fighting mass.

The other women of our party fled down the hill towards us.

'Run, Kate!' Susan hurried past and pulled my mistress forward. I hitched up my skirts and sprinted after her, and to my relief Kate followed us.

But my relief was short-lived. When we emerged from the trees at the crossroads, a large group of hostile-looking women was waiting for us. I skidded to a stop.

They were not women I knew.

One of them picked up a stone.

'Diggers out!' The chant was crystal clear.

The sky filled with the dark stings of flying sticks and stones. A rock glanced my cheek. Kate doubled over to protect her head with her hands.

Susan tried to run again.

'No!' Kate grabbed her and shouted into her terrified face, 'Don't run. We're Diggers remember. Stand together.'

We clasped together then, in a huddle, under the rain of more stones and clods of dry earth. From the corner of my eyes I saw the silhouettes of Mr Grice and his men. They were talking and gesticulating. Mistress Binch was pointing up the hill. So she had told Grice about the meetings in the barn after all. I was about to warn Kate when a clod of stony earth hit me in the face and blinded me.

I panicked, suddenly plunged into darkness and silence.

A pair of hands took me by the shoulders. Kate. She clung on to my waist to stop me running. I blinked, still half-blinded, rubbed my face. Just in time, for the village men were streaming towards us, leaping and yelling something in jubilation. The women who had thrown stones opened their mouths too like braying donkeys.

A scatter of missiles thudded down around us before they took the road in a great crowd, congratulating each other, the men with blood-stained fists, full of jesting and bravado. We watched them disappear around the corner in the direction of Wheathamstead. Mr Grice and Mistress Binch were gone along with them. I hoped to heaven they had not recognised us.

In their wake we stood shivering, the rain pelting down on us, tending our grazes as best we could. One of the women was faint after she had been hit on the temple by a stone. We huddled together but nobody came.

'I'm going to see what's happened.' I set off up the hill, and Kate followed in my wake. We were all subdued, fearful of what we would find when we reached the clearing.

Nothing of the men's hard work remained. The houses were flattened, the fire scattered, our food wasted. But we were relieved to see the men still standing, bedraggled from the rain. Ralph squeezed a bloodied kerchief to a gash on his forehead.

At the sight of us, limping and clutching our cuts and grazes, Ralph hurried over, took Kate by the arm.

Kate told him about the women.

He was angry with himself. 'We should never have let you go alone. I shouldn't have asked you to come. Are you hurt?'

Kate shook her head and looked about her at the broken houses. 'It's ruined. Look at it.'

'Never mind that. Next time we will keep you women folk away until it is established.'

Jacob came over, 'Are you all right?' he asked.

'It looks like you came off the worst,' I said, for one of his eyes was almost closed and his hands were cut and bruised.

He tried to smile, but it obviously hurt.

'They'll not stop us,' Ralph said. 'Right is on our side. How far down do they own this land?' He grabbed up a handful of wet earth, showed it round in front of us. 'To here? Or further down to where our spades reach? Does a mole recognise these boundaries? No, he can go where he wishes on God's land. Are we less than a mole? We who are made in God's likeness? No. We will persevere.'

Ralph looked round expectantly, expecting a cheer, but the men's faces were doubtful.

'Come on, men!'

I felt almost sorry for him.

'We women will be with you Ralph, in spirit, if not in body.' Kate's face shone. 'And I for one I would stand by your side, if you'd only let me.'

The women clapped and whooped and then the men looked a little more convinced. Ralph's next shout, 'Never say die!' was greeted with the cheer he wanted. I saw him look to Kate and beam.

I had to grip tight to my apron and press my lips together to remind myself, she wasn't Kate, the zealous Digger, but Lady Katherine, wife to Sir Thomas Fanshawe. Her servant, Mistress Binch, had incited Soper and his men to destroy what Ralph had built. But there was no doubt Kate meant her words, and it brought a cold chill to my heart.

How could my mistress be so foolish? Love between her and Ralph would be a disaster.

CHAPTER TWELVE

Letters and Lies

That night I sent up a fervent prayer that the Fanshawe men would return soon and that my mistress would behave as a proper wife should and never see Ralph again. Lord help us, if word got out that my mistress had been on the common. Sir Simon would beat her senseless.

Our bruises were hard to explain away. Lady Katherine told Grice she had grazed her hands falling off her horse and that it had kicked me when I went to catch it. I could see he did not quite believe her, but could find no other explanation for the cuts on her hands or my bruised cheek. We were both forbidden to leave the house, or to ride unless he accompanied us, and his servants were to prevent us if we tried to go out. In one way it was a relief, to know my mistress was safe indoors.

Grice busied himself close to Lady Katherine in the main chamber, poring over property deeds and an inventory of goods. Every so often he would ask my mistress rudely what had been spent on vinegar for the polishing, or how much bran the horses ate. His presence meant Lady Katherine and I could have no conversation, and the day was airless. The room grew stuffy and still, except for my mistress's quill moving over the parchment as she copied tracts from the Bible or stitched her sampler.

I saw a thought pass over her face, and she paused with her needle poised over the embroidery. 'Can Ralph read?' she mouthed.

I nodded, already wary.

She smiled thoughtfully, and got out a clean parchment.

Later, Mr Grice fetched maps of the county, and spent a long time tracing the boundaries with his finger and showing Pitman and Rigg routes to Worcester. I feared he was planning the movement of troops and horses for the King's Army, and I immediately regretted the promise I made my father to let him know of any Royalist plans. When I had finished dusting the furniture and rubbing the windows I was dismissed.

When I went up again to repair the fire. Mr Grice and his men had their backs to us and Lady Katherine thrust a neatly-folded letter into my hand.

'For Ralph,' she mouthed.

I was reluctant, and tried to push it away, but Mr Grice turned round, sensing some disturbance and I stuffed the parchment hastily into my skirt waistband.

As I cleaned the rest of the upstairs windows, the letter was like a brand burning my stomach. I toyed with the idea of breaking the seal to see what was in it. But it was one thing giving Mr Grice letters from my mistress to Sir Simon or Thomas Fanshawe, but another handing over something meant for my brother. I'd never do that. I slammed the window shut and picked up my pail.

I was beginning to think it might be a good idea after all if my father could persuade Ralph to join the New Model Army. Then this business with my mistress would stop. But that daft Susan had told Ralph how brave Kate was – that she'd made us all stand up for our rights against the mob of village women. So far from putting Ralph off, the fighting had bonded him to Kate even more. And Kate was just as moon-faced over Ralph.

At ten bells Mr Grice came and summoned me to his chamber as usual.

'Today's correspondence from Lady Katherine,' he said, holding out his hand.

I shook my head and acted stupid on purpose because I did not want to tell him about Ralph or the letter.

'She was writing a letter earlier, I saw her.' Mr Grice gestured to his servant and Pitman took hold of me by the neck with one hand, pinioning me to the wall. I could scarcely breathe, Pitman's fleshy hand pressed against my neck, my pulse throbbed against his thumb. Mr Grice moved in, so his face was so close I could see the sweat on his nose. Instinctively I tried to flinch away, but his eyes bored into mine, as if he knew I was withholding something.

'If she receives any more letters from her husband I want to know. And hers to him are to come straight to me. Do you understand?'

I choked out, 'She gave me no letters.' Pitman tightened his hold so I gasped and struggled.

'None?'

I made a noise, and Pitman pushed me away, with enough force that I fell to my knees on the hard boards. Mr Grice seemed satisfied, but before I could get up he cuffed me a stinging blow on the ear with his boot.

I vowed to keep well out of his way, so the next day I busied myself in the kitchen helping Mistress Binch prepare the meals. In the afternoon I saw his horse was being saddled in the yard. Mistress Binch and I peered out from the kitchen window.

'They're going to inspect the corn mill, so I'm told.'

I breathed a sigh of relief.

'Mind, I hope his servants are well-armed,' Mistress Binch said. 'No-one's safe on the highway. We've had a spate of hold-ups. They're calling him the Silent Highwayman in the village, because he never speaks, just points his pistol at you. The butcher was telling me he's held up the Sheriff, and poor Lady Ann twice, not four miles from here on the London Road. About a month ago, it was.'

'What happened?'

'He just loomed out of the dark, made her hand over her jewellery and coin with a gun pointing at her chest. He wears a hat and a cloth over his face, dark gloves, brown boots. But he never speaks. They say he watches from the woods. Just the thought of those cold eyes watching makes me shiver.'

Brown boots. Just like the dirty ones I'd found in Thomas's closet. Had Lady Katherine befriended an outlaw?

The possibility flared in my imagination, then I dismissed it. I was being fanciful. 'Do you know what he stole from the Lady Ann?'

'Her rings, a bag of florins. He even made her take off a brooch she was wearing.'

'What kind of brooch?'

'Give over with your questions.' She flipped a cloth at me and it stung my cheek. 'How should I know?'

Amethyst, said a little voice in my head, *shaped like a thistle.*

Mistress Binch prodded me with a floury finger to get my attention. 'If you want to ask questions, go and find out when Mr Grice is riding out. There'll be nobody to cook for if he's not in for supper,' she said. 'Take up these fresh scones, see if you can find out what's going on.'

Mr Grice told me he would be out all day visiting a Captain Wentworth. On the way back I took out the letter from Kate to Ralph. Or Lady Katherine to Ralph. I wasn't sure any more who she was. I turned it over in my hands, examined it with a troubled frown. Since Mistress Binch had told me about the Silent Highwayman, an awful thought was brewing, but I pushed it away. It surely couldn't be my mistress. She was an enigma, a puzzle I couldn't make out, there was no doubt about that. But highway robbery? No, she was too much the lady. I remembered then how she'd lugged stones on the common. If she could be Kate, she could be...

I shook my head to rid myself of the thought. Why couldn't she just be satisfied with being a fine lady in this fine house? She had more than most people ever dreamed of; wealth, land, a position.

But deep down, I knew the answer. There was no love in this house. And if I was her, I wouldn't want her family.

'I told you that they'd close up the house,' Mistress Binch said, the next day. 'I knew it. We'll be next out of that door, you mark my words. Quick now, you're to go upstairs, they're waiting.'

The door of an upstairs bedchamber stood open. Grice was there directing his men, Rigg and Pitman, who were carrying out a delicate curved-fronted table. When I glanced through the window I could see a trundle cart, already stacked with the heavy items of furniture, including bedposts and carved linen chests.

The floor was littered with smaller items. Several wicker trunks and leather cases lay open on the dusty floorboards. Mr Grice pointed at these and at the rest of the things on the floor. It was obvious he wanted me to pack them up, so I began, kneeling in the dust to fold up the bed drapes.

Grice stooped awkwardly, leaning on his stick, so he could pocket a few silver items from the heaps on the floor and put others to one side.

I was just pressing the drapes into a chest when I looked up to see Lady Katherine's skirts swish in through the door.

'What's this?' she asked.

'I am clearing this room,' Grice said. We no longer use it, so the contents will be sold.'

'But this was my mother's room.' Lady Katherine looked aghast at the empty chamber.

'Your mother is dead.'

'But –'

'She no longer needs it. It has been left to rot for five years, when someone could have use of it. All the goods deserve a second life. Your step-father's orders.'

'But what about her clothes, her jewellery? Where are they? She would have wanted me to have those, I'm sure.' Lady Katherine bent to look through one of the chests.

'Stop,' Mr Grice said, pointing at her with his stick. 'You are too late. They have already been sold.'

'You sold them?' A hand flew to her mouth, her eyes welled with tears.

'Sir Simon insisted.'

Rigg brushed past and picked up another trunk. 'Wait,' my mistress called. Rigg ignored her so she had to step to the side. She appealed to Mr Grice, 'I know nothing of all this. Surely my husband would have written to tell me. Where are these orders you say you have? Show me the letter.'

'I have not kept it. Why would I? I'm not some woman that hoards all her letters as keepsakes.'

His rudeness made my mistress gasp. 'Now just a minute –'

'Write to Sir Simon yourself. Ask him if you don't believe me.'

My mistress backed away, her tears replaced by determination. 'I will. Believe me, I will. And I will make sure every last item of my mother's is returned to its proper place.'

'If you can find them.' Grice smiled, his lips pressed together. 'They go to auction tomorrow –' He caught sight of me, my eyes fixed intently on his face. He gestured angrily with his stick, pointed at the door. 'You, get out.'

I could not pretend not to understand so I dropped the nightdress I was folding and scurried away.

That night Mr Grice positioned Pitman like a guard outside Lady Katherine's door. He seemed to need little sleep, for when my mistress sent me to get a cup of milk in the middle of the night, he was already on his feet when I pulled open the door.

'Return to bed,' he said, looming over me, 'Mr Grice's orders. Lady Katherine can have her milk in the morning.'

I placed the candle back on the side table, and shook my head at my mistress.

'Pitman won't let me go down.'

'So I am to be a prisoner now in my own home,' she said. 'Well they can't hold me, no matter how they try.'

'It's not right,' I said, 'You are mistress here, not him.' I could have said more but I held my tongue. Mr Grice was up to something. I was sure he had been lying when he said that selling everything was Sir Simon's idea. His words did not match his face, and I knew well enough there had been no letters for Mr Grice from Sir Simon. Only letters for Lady Katherine in Thomas's handwriting. And those, I was forbidden to deliver.

But if I told her now I'd stopped her letters, she'd be furious and so would Mr Grice, and I'd be thrown out of the Manor quicker than lightning. So I kept my mouth firmly shut.

The following day Grice had his servants wrap up the remaining paintings in the hall. Draughts seemed to blow through the corridors, the house grew forlorn and empty.

At least it meant I could be what I was supposed to be – a servant. Lady Katherine was crotchety and short with me, so I was glad to be with Mistress Binch, digging the vegetables, jugging the hare, milking, scrubbing out pots. The kitchen at least was a place of normality and Mistress Binch seemed glad of my help. She stopped shouting at me and her shoulders relaxed.

At mid-day Grice complimented her on the hare stew and she was less surly for the rest of the afternoon.

'Now that's a proper gentleman,' she said. 'One that knows good food when he sees it.'

I grunted. Some gentleman. I had broached him about my wages only that morning and he had dismissed me with a slap and said I'd have them by the end of the week. But his promises were like chaff. He'd promised last week and the week before, and still my pockets were empty.

No sooner were the plates cleared than Mistress Binch got me busy again pressing cheese and making pastry for a tart for the evening meal. She was happy only when she was cooking, I realised. As long as we were making something edible, and as long as I kept chopping and peeling, things would go smoothly.

'You love cooking, don't you?' I said.

She looked at me as though I was foolish. 'Of course. I'm a cook, aren't I?'

She slapped the pastry down on the table and pummelled it flat. 'But I'm starved of good ingredients here. I need a bigger house to cook for. I want to work for Lady Ann. She keeps a good table and there are thirteen servants at her house. I'm wasted here; at least Grice knows good fare when he sees it. Lady Katherine couldn't care whether what I serve her is a boiled egg or a pheasant banquet.'

I had brought out Lady Katherine's letter to Ralph so often I knew it by heart – the elegant single word of my brother's name, the raised blob of red sealing wax with just a thumb print and no proper seal. Of course she couldn't use her fleur-de-lis-seal or he'd know Kate was Lady Katherine straight away.

But it was dangerous to keep the letter. The Fanshawes would have my brother hanged if they knew he had dared to be so familiar with the Lady Katherine.

When I rode up to the common and put the letter into Ralph's hands, he looked at it in amazement. 'From Kate?' he said, 'She can write?' But his face shone from the inside.

Pray God she had put something in the letter to give herself away, so I could rid myself of this ridiculous pretence. She could not blame me, then, could she? I watched as Ralph unfolded the square and screwed up his eyes to read.

'Tell her, 'yes',' he said.

'Yes to what?'

'I'll meet her under the broad oak as she asks.'

'But she –' I stopped. I could not tell him that Grice had now put her practically under lock and key. 'She won't come,' I said.

'Of course she will, or why would she ask? I wish you wouldn't be like this about her.'

'Ralph, she's just leading you a dance, playing with you, she's not...' He folded his arms, his face closed against me. It was hopeless.

'I'll tell her,' I said, 'but I'm right. You'll see.' And I turned Pepper and galloped away before they could miss me at the house.

That night I told my mistress I'd delivered her letter.

'Well?' Lady Katherine's eyes were eager.

'He said yes. But you can't go,' I said, 'Mr Grice's men will be outside.'

'I know,' she said, 'but never fear, they can't hold me here.'

'Please don't,' I said. 'Think of the risk. Your stepfather would kill Ralph if he knew.'

'He's away. He'll never know, not unless you tell him.'

'And there's your husband –'

'Yes, I've written to Thomas, to tell him about Grice selling off my mother's furniture. Maybe he can dissuade Sir Simon. But I'm not sure if my letter will get there in time for him to do anything about it. The mail seems so uncertain – I've had no letters for weeks.'

I reddened and turned away.

When I turned back she was twisting her nightgown in her hands, 'And anyway, I'm not sure any more that I want Thomas to come home.'

I poured water into the ewer with a hollow pain in my chest. I knew precisely where the letter to her husband was, and that it would never get there because I'd given it to Grice myself. To cover my awkwardness I asked, 'What will happen when your husband gets back?'

She ignored my question. 'Since you came, everything's changed. You brought some magic with you. It gives me a strange feeling, as if the ground is shaking under my feet. I don't know who I am any more. All I know for certain is that I like the way Ralph looks at me, as if I'm a person worth seeing. I see something in his eyes, something I can't escape. And he's handsome isn't it he?'

I made a face. To me he was just my brother with his too-big boots and foolish crazes. 'When are you meeting?' I said.

She hesitated, looked at me as if weighing me up. 'Tuesday,' she said.

A few days away yet.

'I think I'll undress now,' she said. She went to the window and stood a moment, before drawing the drapes against the waning light. It was unlike Lady Katherine to be weary, she was always full of barely-compressed energy.

I lay down on the floor by her bed, but could not sleep. Too many things raced around my mind. But the housework had taken its toll and after much tossing and turning, I fell into a deep slumber.

When I woke it was dark, but the white linen of Lady Katherine's bed shone out. She was not in her bed. I sat up and peered round the room. Where was she? When I pulled open the drapes the moon gleamed in at the window and it was almost bright as day. Yet there was still no sign of Lady Katherine. I went to the door and opened it a crack.

Curse it, the servant was still there, his bulk sprawled on a chair across the doorway. So she hadn't gone that way.

The door to the adjoining room was locked, and the key was gone. I searched her dressing chamber before spotting the obvious. Lady Katherine's silks and satins were still on the trunk by the bed, and her nightdress was on the coverlet.

How had she sneaked past Mr Grice's man without her clothes? I rushed to the window and looked out. There was no way down, there was only a drop to the ground that made me dizzy. I squinted into the darkness.

It was a full moon. A dark shadow against the trees was given away by the blaze of the horse. The way the man rode was familiar – the set of his shoulders, his upright posture. I remembered the dropped glove, the brooch, her husband's wet cloak.

It wasn't a man at all. It was my mistress.

Where was she going? How had she got out? If she didn't come back before morning, I'd be left trying to explain to Mr Grice what had become of her. I wrapped myself in the coverlet and sat up on her bed, something I would never have dared to do when I first came to the Manor. I faced the door, watching for her return.

I did not intend to sleep, but I must have dozed a little. When the door swung open the light from the hall jerked me awake. It was Mistress Binch, with a tray of warmed ale for my mistress. She took one look and shouted at me to get off the bed and get down to the kitchen. I grasped from her gesticulations that she assumed Lady Katherine was in the dressing room, and I'd better tell her to hurry and get dressed. Mr Grice awaited her at breakfast.

When Misrtess Binch had gone, I raced across the hall and up the servants' stairs, my arms tight across my chest, terrified I'd be caught in just my chemise. In my room I threw on my skirt and bodice and ran to the kitchen. It would be my fault when my mistress's absence was discovered, and I feared what Mr Grice would do. By the time I arrived breathlessly in the kitchen the porridge had already been served and Mistress Binch was scrambling eggs.

'Sorry,' I said, still tucking my hair into my new coif.

She thrust the covered dish into my hands, eying me with disapproval. 'Quick, before it goes cold.'

I grabbed the handles and went up.

Lady Katherine was sitting at the table, her face pink and flushed, but dressed like a lady should be, not even out of breath. I stopped dead, unable to believe it. I put down the dish and saw her unfold a napkin on her knee.

My Grice helped himself, noticing nothing amiss. 'The salt, Chaplin.' He mimed shaking the salt cellar over his food.

I did not register what he meant; I was too busy watching my mistress.

'I said, the salt.' He raised his eyebrows. 'God pre-serve us from idiot servants.'

Lady Katherine stifled a smile.

CHAPTER THIRTEEN

A Hiding Place

Later after I'd aired Lady Katherine's bed I made another search of the room. I prowled round the edges of the chamber but could see no other way out. She could not have walked through the wall like a ghost, could she? I paced back and forth in annoyance, until I realised one floorboard was shorter and had more spring than the rest. I pressed on it with my boot again and it shifted. Squatting, I prised it up with my fingers and felt underneath. I touched something rough. A hessian bag.

I pulled it out and loosened the drawstring. My breath almost stopped. Inside the light caught the glint of gold coins and the sparkle of jewellery. The weight of it alone told me there was probably enough here to buy six strips of land.

My heart made a double beat. I'd have to tell someone. I glanced over my shoulder before I emptied out the contents into my apron. There was the thistle brooch belonging to Lady Ann, from the night Sir Simon got out the birch. I'd recognise that anywhere. And another necklace with stones that could be diamonds. Only I'd never seen a diamond, so I couldn't be sure they weren't just glass. They were stolen, I knew. But if I told someone, would they believe me? They might think I'd stolen them myself. Huh, I knew enough of the world to know it was always the servant's fault.

I could tell Jacob; after all his father was the constable. But if they believed me, what then? What would happen to Lady Katherine? I could not bear the thought of her being locked up. Her life was hard enough.

The again, I could keep it. If these were real diamonds there would be enough for me to leave here, and more than enough to buy a plot of land for Mother. But I dare not. It was too large a risk. Lady Katherine would know it was me and I'd be punished. Stealing from your employer was a hanging offence. And if you did something bad, I knew well enough the punishment would come quick and sure, like it had five years before. The Devil would blow on the misdeed with his bellows and the evil would come back tenfold.

I bundled it all back and trod hard onto the board to make it lie flat. My hands shook when I stood up and my heart was pattering very fast. I hastened from the room to put more space between me and the stolen hoard.

As I laid the table my thoughts rambled round in circles trying to make sense of it all. If my mistress was what I thought she was, she was an outlaw and a felon.

She would bring us all down with her if she was caught. But one thing I did know. I had to stop her meeting Ralph on Tuesday.

But on Tuesday night Grice kept me a long time in his room. His leg was worse and every time I rose to go, he asked me to fetch more water or more linen. I gritted my teeth and did the dressing as fast as I could.

'Fat-witted girl!' he grumbled. 'It's all wrinkled. I can't walk with it like that. Fetch more linen and do it again. That spoiled dressing can come out of your wages.'

I hared to the linen press and came back panting with a pillowslip which I tore into strips. 'For heaven's sake!' he said. 'You make an infernal noise everywhere you go. It gives everyone a headache. There's no hurry.' I nearly wept with frustration.

Finally he let me go, and I bolted up to my mistress's room. Pitman was already stationed at the door and he tried to bar my way, intent on pinching my bottom as I passed him, but I was too quick, and slammed the door behind me.

The room was empty.

I let out a roar of disappointment. She had out-foxed me. It was too late. I could find no other way out, but somewhere out there my brother was meeting my mistress and I was trapped indoors unable to do anything about it.

And Mr Grice had said I was always noisy. I couldn't hear how much din I made so he was probably right. I wondered how my voice sounded. Did I speak too loud? I sagged. Ralph's face had glowed with the idea of meeting Kate. But she was not simple Kate at all. She was a royalist lady and a highway robber and Lord knows what else.

The image of Ralph's smiling face would not go away, though I pummelled on the bed in frustration. Jealousy squeezed its claws into me. I wished Jacob would look at me the way Ralph looked at Kate, but I always did something bird-brained whenever Jacob was near me. It was as if he brought out the boggarts and the clumsy spirits from their hiding places and they were all teasing me. I was stupid. I always had been. Only someone like me could leave a candle alight next to a curtain and forget it was there.

That was the end of my family's comfortable life. Nobody ever said it was my fault. But I knew. And even though I'd been punished, I still felt responsible. If only I could I'd turn back time I'd snuff the candle so hard the wax would splash right up to my elbow. Then we'd still be in our panelled chamber with its polished tables and turkey rugs. And I would still be able to play the virginals instead of scrubbing floors.

Next morning, Lady Katherine had not reappeared by the time I had to begin my kitchen duties, but she was coming down the stairs as I was going up. Of course I stood to one side.

'Did you meet Ralph?' I said, even though it was not my place to ask.

'Yes,' she whispered, her eyes sparkling. 'He was asking if I have any kin to stop me joining them in their community. I told him there was no-one.'

'But it's not true.' I could hardly get out the words, my tongue seemed to stick in my mouth.

'I want to be with him. If I could, I'd be his wife.'

Had I heard her right? 'His wife?' I asked.

She took hold of my hands and squeezed them tight, nodded her head.

'You can't.' My heart seemed to freeze in my chest. 'You are already married.'

'Ralph asked me. Or rather he hinted as much. And he's going to meet me again tonight.' And she whisked past me down the stairs and into the chamber where Mr Grice was waiting.

I could not move. I never believed she would go this far. I would have to do something. But what? That was the question.

CHAPTER FOURTEEN

Truth Will Out

I was determined to run to Ralph to tell him who Kate was, but I couldn't get away. It was laundry day and Mistress Binch kept me so busy I couldn't get a minute of free time. I ground my teeth in frustration. And the next day, just as I was about to slip away I was called by Mr Grice.

'We are riding to the notary in St Albans,' he said. 'You will accompany us.'

I looked to Lady Katherine. She was grim-faced and white. There was an atmosphere as though an argument had just taken place, a slight bristling of the air.

Grice hoisted me by the arm and took me to the window. He pointed to my pony which was just being saddled. 'Riding. Out. You will come,' he said. He obviously still thought I was dim in the wits and Lady Katherine did not speak up for me.

Needless to say, Mistress Binch was not pleased she was to do all the chores herself that day and it earned me yet another black look.

Pitman had to give Mr Grice a leg up onto his horse which turned to nip at his foot. I hoped the bad-tempered animal would manage to bite him and get a mouthful of wood. The sun beat down on my back as we rode. Rigg brought up the rear, then me on little Pepper, behind a silent Lady Katherine. Mr Grice and Pitman rode ahead of us to lead the way.

The St Albans road was notorious for thieves and I was glad Rigg had a flintlock pistol in his belt, and both servants had swords though they looked as though they were guarding Lady Katherine, rather than protecting us from brigands - just something about the way they watched her. Lady Katherine looked elegant as she rode - her swinging curls, the flowing skirts. There was no trace whatsoever of Kate, the girl who had shovelled earth with her bare hands. Nor could I imagine her holding up a coach in the dead of night. I was surely mistaken. This young woman in the green riding habit looked every inch a lady.

On the way I asked the servant Rigg why we were going into town and he told me my mistress was needed to sign some documents.

The fields shimmered in the heat haze and sweat trickled down my forehead. Flies buzzed around the horses' ears. In the town we tethered our horses outside the notary's shop, which was half-timbered and gloomy, its small leaded windows like half-closed eyes.

I waited outside with Pitman who smiled at me in a leering way that made me uncomfortable. It had happened before and it made me want to fold my arms across my chest to stop him from looking.

Mr Grice and my mistress had only been gone a few moments when Lady Katherine shot out of the door all in a flurry, and put her foot in the stirrup to mount her horse. Mr Grice was right behind. He grasped her by the waist to pull her down.

'Leave go!' Lady Katherine's face was white and angry. I leapt forward to help her but Rigg shoved me away with his rough red hands. My mistress struggled, but Rigg and Pitman held her fast.

'You will sign,' Mr Grice said.

'No!' She kicked out at him, and he staggered backwards, losing balance. A puff of dust as he landed heavily on his back. He immediately tried to get to his feet again, but his wooden foot could get no purchase.

'I won't sign.' Lady Katherine stood over him in defiance. 'The King will win and my husband will return.'

'Help me, you fools.' Pitman and Rigg levered Grice to his feet. A vein stood out on Grice's forehead. 'The King cannot win,' Mr Grice said, his lips small with suppressed rage. 'The Scots failed him. Sir Simon fears his lands will be forfeit. He wants me to take possession of them in case he is captured. He will need to flee to avoid execution. That's why he sent me these signed agreements.'

'No. I won't sign away a single acre, not even a blade of grass! Not until I've spoken to my husband.'

'It is a simple signature. Your stepfather has signed them already. You must witness the papers; that is all.'

'You cannot force me.'

Grice lost patience. 'You think I can't? How about a little hunting accident when nobody is looking?' I was not sure I had heard him right until he drew out his pistol and fingered it thoughtfully. He pressed it gently to the side of Lady Katherine's neck. She flinched away from it, but he pushed it harder. I did not know if it was loaded. He gestured for the men to take her back inside.

'You would not...' She laughed, thinking it a joke. But then she looked up into his face and her words died away.

They manoeuvred her through the door, the pistol still at her neck.

I walked away from the door shakily, brushed dust from my skirts although they did not really need it. But my hands needed to do something because I could not believe what I had just seen.

I could run away. But I didn't want to leave Lady Katherine alone.

Pitman came back out and grinned at me in a conspiratorial way, but I ignored him. I could not sit, I was too shaken. He made a lewd gesture poking a finger at me and I went away to the churchyard to wait on a bench out of the sun.

The wait seemed interminable but finally the sundial on the church tower read two o'clock and Mr Grice emerged, holding Lady Katherine by the arm. She was dry-eyed and blank-faced. We mounted in an atmosphere sharp as a pike and set off back to the house. This time the bridle of Lady Katherine's horse was tethered and held by the servants, as if she might gallop away.

After we had gone past the turnpike toll and paid our pennies she said to me, 'You may leave me if you wish, find another place. I will give you a reference.'

I could not answer, because the road improved and Grice's horse broke into a canter and we had to keep up. As we approached the village we had to pass Norland Common where the Diggers had built their settlement.

Grice slowed his horse to a trot. A fallen branch from a large oak tree was almost blocking the way.

Two young men were there on the road, bare-chested, swinging their axes to cut it. As we got closer they stepped to one side to let us pass.

I stiffened in the saddle. A surge of recognition. It was Ralph and Jacob.

I kicked Pepper on, urging him forward until I was alongside Lady Katherine, 'Mistress!' I shouted, frantic, but she did not hear me and there was no time to give another warning. I feared they would call to her and then Grice would arrest them both.

We had to slow to go round the tree and it was as if the world slid to a standstill. My brother doffed his hat as was the custom to passing noblemen, and then he saw me. His face broke into a smile and he lifted his hand to wave. His eyes glanced to Lady Katherine and stopped, fixed there.

We were passing them now. Lady Katherine's head whipped round, I saw her lower her eyes, bring one hand up to cover her face. But it was too late. Ralph was behind us, standing in the middle of the road, one hand outstretched as if to call back the Kate he knew.

CHAPTER FIFTEEN

Dark Passage

Mr Grice galloped ahead and all I could think of was my brother's expression, as if he had been slapped. Lady Katherine's cheeks had flared into two bright spots of crimson, but I could not get close enough to speak to her.

Grice dismounted at the front door and gestured for us to fall in behind him. As we entered the sun was cut by shadow. I went over to Lady Katherine but she could not stand still; she paced the floor folding and re-folding her gloves.

'You have mud on your hem,' Grice said. 'You may change from your riding habit if you wish.'

Lady Katherine threw me a distressed look.

'I will help the mistress change,' I said.

Mr Grice gave me a thin smile. 'I expect you both back downstairs forthwith.'

We made a grateful escape to my mistress's chamber.

It wasn't until we were in the dressing room that she said, 'It was Ralph, wasn't it?'

'Yes.'

'Do you think he saw?'

I nodded. I was relieved that I didn't have to pretend any more, except that I could see the misery on milady's face as she unfastened her riding habit and let it drop. It made me tearful to see her. She hugged herself, and her knuckles showed white. When she turned so that I could unlace the bodice, there were still raised scabs where she had been beaten. It softened my heart.

She stepped out of her petticoats and held them out to me. 'I just wanted someone to like me for who I was. Not because I'm Lady Fanshawe or because I have money or position. Ralph says the Diggers are like a family. I've never had a family. My mother died when I was eight years old.'

I rested my hand on her shoulder to comfort her.

'Can you imagine – nobody locks doors in the Digger community, he says, because they hold all goods in common. Such a relief, not to be judged by your fortune. Was it so foolish of me to dream of a different life?'

'No milady. But my Mother always says, people must do their duty according to their station.'

'But station is just a word. Like the way they call me a lady, yet I have no goods to speak of, no privileges, no position. I am just a bag of coins to be raked through by any man who can get close enough to threaten me. Like

Grice.' She took my hand in entreaty, 'I didn't mean what I said on the road. You won't leave me, will you?'

I pulled my hand away. 'Grice is dangerous. He scares me.'

'My stepfather sent Grice some signed documents. To sign over the tenancies to him so Parliament can't take them if the Royalists lose. The corn mill, the weaver's cottages, parcels of land. He thinks my stepfather will need to hide abroad. It seems premature, when we don't know yet what will happen, and it's my inheritance. I don't like it.'

I had seen no letters from Sir Simon, but I did not dare say so.

I put her gloves in the drawer. 'I expect Grice is only following orders. But to threaten you like that, it's not right.'

'None of them care for me. But Ralph – he's different, he thought I was just a farm girl. He liked me because of who I am.'

'But you are Lady Katherine.'

'No, you don't understand,' she said, shaking her head, 'I'm not. I'm Kate on the inside.'

We could not talk more because the door swung open.

'Your brother's here,' Mistress Binch said, glaring. 'Flaming cheek of it. Just to knock on the door and expect me to run round after you.' Her forehead was perspiring from having to come up the stairs to fetch me.

I glanced at Lady Katherine before ducking away under Mistress Binch's arm, through the open door. I sped downstairs. Ralph was at the back door; he must have come straight over, for his shirt was stuck to his back with sweat.

'Tell me I'm wrong,' he said.

I did not reply, but my eyes could not meet his.

'It was Lady Katherine Fanshawe you were riding out with today, wasn't it?'

I nodded miserably.

'Not Kate?'

'No.' My face must have told him everything. He balled his fist and slammed it into the wall, I saw his lips spit out curses. 'You stupid girl.' His eyes when they turned to me were full of pain. 'You've ruined everything. How could you? She's our enemy. Her and all her land-grabbing family. You helped her, didn't you, to disguise herself as one of us?' He took hold of my arm, shook it, his thumbs digging into my flesh so I winced. 'The Diggers trusted me – and now it's my fault. It was her wasn't it? She sent people to destroy the Diggers' houses –'

'It wasn't her, it was Mistress Binch, she was spying on us. She was at the Common, I saw her talking to Mr Grice –'

'You deceived me. How could you do that to me? To your own brother? Here was I thinking Kate was bonny and clear and good, and all the time she was calculating and spying on us.' He turned as if he would walk away, strode back and forth to quiet his own restlessness. Finally he turned to me with a wounded expression, 'I thought she liked me, but I'll bet she despised me. She's probably been laughing at me the whole time.'

'No, she wasn't. She admired you. Her family treat her like a beast. She only wanted –'

'Why? Why did you bring her?'

'She said...I knew I'd lose my position if I didn't.'

He shot me a look of ice. 'She's a viper. You're leaving, come on, I'll take you home.' And he began to tug on my arm.

'Hoy!' Mr Grice and his servants rounded the corner. 'What's this? Who are you and what do you want?'

'Ralph Chaplin. Abigail's brother. She's leaving.'

Mr Grice shot me a displeased look as though his mouth was full of vinegar. I expected him to dismiss me on the spot, but he surprised me.

'No she is not,' he said. 'She has not given notice. She will get no pay and no reference.'

'Please, Ralph,' I begged, 'don't make a fuss. I need that reference. Please, just go. We'll talk later.'

I was scared Grice would throw Mother off the Fanshawe estate. And I'd worked months, I couldn't bear the thought that I'd get no pay and it would all be for nothing.

'You are not working for the Fanshawes.' Ralph was angry now, tell-tale signs of red flaring on his neck.

I was begging him, hopping from foot to foot. He didn't understand anything. 'Please Ralph, go home. I'll come and explain later –'

Grice did not wait for me to get the words out, 'Remove this trespasser from my land,' he ordered. The servants moved in to take Ralph by the elbows. 'Chaplin, inside. Now.'

I gave Ralph an anguished look, bobbed my head and hurried inside. Grice followed me, pulled the door shut after us, and limped his way purposefully upstairs. Mistress Binch simply stared, unable to believe Mr Grice had actually been in her kitchen. I ran to the kitchen window and was just in time to see the servants manhandle Ralph down the drive until he finally freed a fist and punched Pitman in the eye.

A few moments later he ran off into the copse, leaving Pitman still floundering on his back in the drive with Rigg trying to help him up. I pressed my hand to my forehead and sighed. Trouble - this could only mean more trouble.

Sure enough, that night when I was dressing his foot Mr Grice said, 'Your brother hit my servant.'

'Yes. I mean, no. I don't know Sir.'

Mr Grice terrified me. I could not get the image out of my mind, of him pressing the pistol to Lady Katherine's neck. He examined me through shrewd eyes. 'You will not see your brother again and you will be obedient to me. Do you understand? Then I might consider keeping you on and giving you a reference.'

I inclined my head, kept my eyes fixed on his lips where white spittle had dried to a crust.

'The constable will deal with your brother.'

I opened my mouth to protest, but realised it would do me no good and closed it again.

'Unruly tenants will not be tolerated.'

'No Sir,' I said.

I could not speak to Lady Katherine until it was time for her to retire that night. Mistress Binch kept me busy and Mr Grice would not let my mistress out of his sight. I was miserable, worrying about what would happen to Ralph. When I went up that night with Lady Katherine's evening drink of hot mulled ale she was waiting for me, just inside her door, as I knew she would be.

'What did he say?' she asked. I knew she meant Ralph.

'He hit one of the servants. And now Grice will send the constable to arrest him, all because of you and your tomfool disguises.' I crashed the tray down on the table. 'What am I going to do? Ralph blames me for lying to him.'

'I'll speak to Mr Grice,' she said.

But we both knew that was hopeless.

I had a sudden urge to hurt her. 'Ralph never wants to see you again,' I said.

I saw the words sink in and her eyes turn shiny. 'Fetch me paper, I'll write to him.'

'He won't read it. And anyway, I won't deliver it. Have you no idea what you've done? Ralph says you've betrayed the Diggers and all he's worked for, that it was you who roused up the villagers against him.'

'It's not true! You've got to tell him!'

'He won't listen.' A wave of emotion engulfed me. I wanted to strike her. I choked out, 'It's my fault he says, for lending you my clothes. You've come between me and my brother, and I'll never forgive you.'

I blundered from the room. I could not trust myself not to cry. A sixth sense told me my mistress was calling after me but I did not turn.

In the kitchen I helped Mistress Binch wipe down the table as she always did last thing at night. My heart was heavy and my head buzzing as if it was a nest to a thousand bees. Ralph had always been my main ally against my sister Elizabeth and the world in general. He'd always had confidence in me; that I could do things other girls could. Now he was blaming me for this whole mess and it hurt.

I dragged the churns out ready for the morning milk and as I did so a little kitten nosed around the corner of the door then came and twined around my feet.

I squatted and spoke to him softly and rubbed his gingery head. He pressed his nose into my hand. Such long whiskers for such a small creature. I found a few drops of milk in the churns and tipped them out for him. Before long he let me pick him up. He felt so lovely and trusting it brought tears to my eyes.

A tap on the shoulder. 'Lady Katherine wants you,' it was Pitman.

I dodged away from him. I could not refuse to go, so I tucked the squirming kitten under my arm and climbed reluctantly up the stairs to Lady Katherine's room.

She was sitting by the window in her nightdress, but stood when I came in. She had been crying, her eyes were puffy and her nose red.

'I'm sorry,' she said, 'I did not mean to be the cause of trouble between you and Ralph.' She saw the kitten struggling in my arms. 'What's that?'

'Mistress Binch said we used to have a cat to keep down the mice.' It wasn't strictly true, but I wanted to keep him.

'Let me see.'

I placed the kitten on the ground and he padded towards her. She knelt and called to him, 'Puss, puss!' he went to her hands and she looked up delighted despite herself. 'What's his name?'

'He hasn't got one yet. He's only one of the farm cats. A she-cat's just had a litter.'

'I know, I'll call him after the Digger leader, what's his name?'

'You mean Winstanley? It's a daft name. You can't call him that.' I was still angry, unable to drop my irritation at her. Yet the kitten would melt anyone's heart. 'Anyway, just look at him, he's so little, and Winstanley was a General for Parliament. Anyway Mr Grice would never stand for it.'

'All the more reason.' She tried to scoop the kitten up but he skittered under the drapes of the bed. 'Here, Winstanley,' she said.

It seemed such a big name for such a little cat that I began to giggle. Soon we were both laughing until our sides ached. After we had recovered she brought out a ribbon and I dangled it before him and we watched Winstanley try to pat it with his paws and chase after it when I pulled it out of sight beneath my skirts.

When Winstanley settled to sleep on Lady Katherine's bed, she went and sat on her chair by the window ready for me to unbraid her hair.

I took out the brush and began to tease her ringlets into order. She sat very still, unlike the Lady Katherine I knew. In the looking glass on the stand I saw that her face was tired, empty.

'I doesn't make sense,' she said. 'I thought Mr Grice was for Sir Simon, for the King, but now I don't know any more. I don't trust him. He's turned bitter. And do you know, I care not a groat for any of them – King, Parliament, all this fighting. It's all just words. The only person I really cared for was Ralph, and now everything is ruined,' she said.

A tear rolled down her cheek. She had not cried when she was bullied by her step-father, or by Grice, but here she was crying over my brother.

She turned and took hold of my hand. 'Please – humour Grice and do as he says.' She wiped her face with her sleeve. 'Don't give him the slightest reason to make you leave. If you go I will have no friend left in the world.'

I was touched by this admission of friendship.

She carried on, 'He says the King will lose to Parliament. Sir Simon fears Thomas will be transported or executed and his land forfeit to Cromwell. That is why we must transfer the estate to Grice. I could write to Thomas to protest, but the mail takes so long,' she said. 'And Thomas is useless, he will only do what Sir Simon wants. Sir Simon is as bad as Grice, I do not want to remind him of my existence.'

'How can they be so certain Parliament will win?'

'I don't know. Letters arrive for Grice every day. I watch out in case there are letters from Thomas to tell me he is returning. But I have heard nothing.'

It was time to confess. I did not dare meet her eyes. I said, 'No letter has come from Sir Simon addressed to Mr Grice, I know that for certain.'

She turned. 'What do you mean?'

I blurted, 'Mr Grice asks me to meet the messengers and bring all the correspondence to him. And there has never been a letter addressed to him from your stepfather. I would know, because I recognise his hand.'

'But Mr Grice said —'

'I know, but I think he has signed all those papers himself.' I told her about the forged signatures. Her eyes widened in disbelief. Finally I confessed to her, 'all your mail to your husband goes to him, and any mail for you never gets past Grice.'

Now she stood up. I cringed, knowing what was coming.

But she did not shout or rail at me. Instead she was thoughtful. 'Why? Why doesn't he want me to write to my husband?'

I stood sheepishly, hung my head. 'I don't know.'

'But you're going to find out, aren't you,' she said, her old determination back. 'You owe me that much. Go to his room and bring me his letters.'

The thought of sneaking into Grice's room made my palms sweat and my stomach curdle. What if he caught me? Servants caught stealing were branded, or worse. But when I went to look, Grice had already retired to his chamber. Rigg was stationed in the hall and told me to go back to bed.

When I returned to my mistress's chamber empty-handed she was not pleased. She paced the floor, and grew impatient with me when I tried to help her wash.

To tell the truth, we were both like cats on hot bricks – except for Winstanley, who was curled up on the satin eiderdown like a little prince.

It was Tuesday, the night Ralph had arranged to meet Kate. I guessed my mistress might try to go out to apologise or try to reason with him. Whether he would even come – well, that I did not know. But I was determined to stay awake just in case.

A single rushlight still burned above the fireplace, as she knew I was wary of the dark. It must have been after midnight when from the corner of my eye I saw the flash of sheets being thrown back. A moment later, when I half-opened my eyes, Lady Katherine's bed was empty. I did not stir but watched her dark shadow move round the room. She was dressing. This time in her own riding habit. I saw another chink of light as she opened the door to the landing, but then closed it again.

She came over towards where I lay before the fire so I closed my eyes tight and pretended to be asleep. The hem of her gown brushed past my ear, I felt the floor-boards slight movement as she passed. When I opened my eyes she was gone. I looked cautiously before sitting up. I crept out of bed and opened the door again quietly but Pitman was there as usual, his head nodding, his chair blocking her exit. So she hadn't gone that way. Perplexed, I tried the door to her husband's room again. Locked.

I dressed in a panic, throwing on my skirts and bodice. The window was still tight shut. The kitten was scratching at the side of the fireplace and I went over to pull him away. A draught - a slight movement of air where he was scratching.

I went down on my hands and knees in the hearth and saw a wooden door set back behind the lintel. It was painted dark grey to match the stone. When I looked more closely there was a hole in it near the shadowed top for my fingers. I pulled and it swung open.

Beyond lay a dark passageway.

The kitten disappeared into its gloom, but I could not go after him, not without a light. I was afraid of where it went, of being shut in. I took the rushlight from the mantel and shielding its glow with my fingers held it up inside the passage. No cobwebs, so it must be in regular use. A priest hole, perhaps. I had heard of these places where priests hid when they were fleeing King James's men, in the time of my grandmother.

This was it. How she got out. Down the narrow stairs I hurried, as quick as I dared.

At the bottom of the stairs the roof grew lower. A shiver of fear rippled up my spine. I had to crouch to get through another small door. I put my eye to the hand hole and saw the lower shelves and familiar books of the reading room. Tentatively I pushed and the door hinged open until I emerged from the side of the inglenook into the empty room. It was only a few steps down the corridor to the back stairs to the kitchen. By the embers from the fire I saw the kitten had found his way there too and was waiting by the back door, his mouth opened in a miaow.

There was barely a sliver of moon and the night was black as ink. I hesitated, heart hammering. But then I glimpsed movement on the drive.

'Milady?' I called, taking a few steps forward.

The kitten shot away from me towards the stable, back to his family probably. I tottered into the darkness, with my rushlight cupped in my hands.

They had said the broad oak, so she would go there first I was sure. But I doubted if Ralph would still come to meet her.

I could see nothing. I crept my way around the side of the house, praying my eyes would soon accustom themselves to the dark. The oak was across the field in the patch of grass away from the house. I set off towards it, hoping to catch a glimpse of Lady Katherine's petticoats.

A gust of wind. The rushlight guttered, leaving me alone in the dark. Blackness dropped round me like a hangman's hood.

My chest constricted; I couldn't breathe. Thoughts of the ghostly monk flooded my mind. Terrified, I swivelled to see what was behind me. The dark reflections of trees in the house windows were the only things I could see. They were like claws. Something brushed my face. I felt a scream come from my throat before I plunged back towards the safety of the house and in through the kitchen door. I closed it fast behind me, leant against it, panting.

It was only a leaf, blowing from the tree. Only that; not ghosts or demons or witches. I knew that now. But I couldn't do it. Couldn't steel myself to go back out there to that black silent world. Shame burned in my throat. Fifteen years old and still afraid of the dark.

I poked at the dying embers of the fire, threw on some tinder and watched it flare up, casting my giant shivering shadow on the ceiling. My hands shook as I added more kindling to the growing blaze. Fires always brought me sorrow as well as comfort.

I stayed there in front of the fire, unable to bring myself to go back up to Lady Katherine's room, for I would have to go the way I came, through the tomb-like passageway, and I just could not. I would wait here, for Lady Katherine must come back this way.

A draught on my cheek made me sit up. Lady Katherine closed the door stealthily, but clutched her hand to her throat when she saw the fire lit and me before it waiting.

She brought her hand to her eyes as if to disguise the fact they were red and swollen.

'He didn't listen,' I said.

Her expression told me I was right.

'Did you ride out to find him? To the Diggers?' She did not reply, but nodded her head. 'I said he wouldn't. He wouldn't listen to me either.'

She sat down on the stool next to me. 'I told him I would give everything up if he would let me join them. But he turned me away. Cast me out in front of everyone. Jacob told me they never turned anyone away.' Her words were choppy, as if they choked her.

'Here, sit by the fire,' I said. 'We must whisper or we'll wake Mr Grice and the servants.'

She sat on a small stool close to the fire. 'He was so cold. Not like the Ralph I knew. He said I would be a millstone around their necks. That a *lady* such as I would never have the strength necessary for such a hard life. Such a sneering tone he had. He never wants to see me again. He told me I was a curse, a bringer of ill-fortune.'

'He's hurt, that we deceived him. And maybe he fears you will draw attention to them from the landowners and the Sherriff.'

'You know him, you must help me, find some way to persuade –'

'I can't. And you can't make me. Not any more. Because I know something about you that nobody else knows.'

She fastened me with a sharp look like a bodkin.

I stood up to face her, hoping my hunch was right. 'I know where you go at night in your husband's clothes.'

'I don't know what you mean,' she said, but her shifting eyes told me that she did.

'I know who you are and what you do, that you ride out at night as the Silent Highwayman. You go out through the priest's hiding place. You have no hold over me now, because I will tell Mr Grice unless you leave my brother alone.'

'You know nothing,' she said. 'You are just a stupid deaf servant girl. Who would believe you?' She swirled her cloak around her shoulders and swept out of the kitchen upstairs into the darkness of the house.

I did not follow her.

CHAPTER SIXTEEN

Mercenaries' Gold

The next day I was so tired I was almost asleep on my feet. Lady Katherine did not send for me, and I did not dare go up to her. But Grice's man, Pitman, summoned me as I was elbow-deep in greasy dishes. I was expecting to get my notice and was prepared to be bold and ask for my wages. But when I got upstairs Grice held out a sealed letter.

'Do you know The Green Man?' he said, mouthing the words carefully.

I nodded, still wiping my arms on my apron, and he passed the letter over.

'Take this to Captain Wentworth and bring me his reply so that I know it has arrived. You may take the pony.'

'Yes Sir.' I stared down at the letter.

'Go then! Wentworth at the Green Man.'

I remembered to curtsey before going out of the room. As I passed I saw my mistress coming the other way so I hastily tucked the letter into my bodice and lowered my eyes.

She did not speak as we passed and her icy look gave me a sharp pang under my ribs. We could have been friends, if she'd really been Kate. Once or twice we had laughed together like friends. But I did not know how things lay between us now, whether she would keep me in her employ. I suspected not, and I feared that in the end I would get no reference and no other mistress would take me without one.

There was one thing I did know though, and that was that I needed to find out what was in Mr Grice's letter. I owed it to Father. Wentworth was a Parliament man – something I didn't know until yesterday when Mistress Binch told me. I'd always assumed that the Captain was a Royalist and I hadn't wanted to get involved. But now everything about Grice was suspicious. Why would Grice be writing to a Parliament Captain?

I creaked open the door to the study and hurried to Lady Katherine's writing desk. I feared the drawer would be locked, but it slid open easily.

When I looked down I saw a pair of lady's flintlock pistols nestled in an open velvet case – polished steel with mother-of-pearl handles. My breath caught in my throat. So these must be what my mistress used in her night-time raids. They were finely chiselled and engraved, quite beautiful. *And probably deadly*, I thought.

I avoided touching them and took out her ladyship's seal and some sealing wax and slipped it into my purse. Her seal would have to do – Grice's own seal was on his ring and he never took it off.

As I came out, my mistress was coming back with her embroidery frame and called after me, but I pretended not to hear and raced away down the stairs.

I saddled Pepper and set off towards Wheathamstead, but instead of going straight to the Green Man I rode up to the common. The place was deserted. The trees were still, even the clouds hung motionless above. The houses had been abandoned half-built, and I had to search before I found Ralph, propped against a silver birch, his spade laid off to one side.

'Where is everyone?' I asked.

'They've given up. When I told them this morning I wasn't for carrying on.'

'Oh Ralph.' I dismounted and tied up the pony. 'Why? What happened? Is it Father? Are you going to join the army?'

'I hadn't the heart for it. I got up this morning and looked at it, and it just seemed too big a task somehow. I've just lost the will to do it. I'm going to do as father asked – fight for Parliament.'

'Is it because of Kate?'

'No, of course not.' His reply was too emphatic. 'I don't want to talk about her. I can't believe you would do that to us, Abi. It made me ashamed. How could I tell all my friends? Anyway it's over.'

'Why? Why give it all up after the trouble you've been through?'

'I felt bad about Father. I don't like to fall out with him. He says the Royalist Army is on its way south and this will be the last stand against the King and they need every man. It will end the fighting for good if we win.'

'But where will you stay, if you are giving up the Diggers? Will you go back home?'

'No. I want my independence. Jacob's offered me a space on his floor. Then I'll go wherever the troops go, I suppose.'

'What about all the things you said about true freedom, and every man having land in common?'

'That was before,' he said bitterly. He stood up and pointed at the rough foundations of his house. 'Look at it. It is not a dream you could offer any decent girl, is it?'

I knew he meant Kate. That he had suddenly seen himself through the eyes of a lady and found himself lacking.

'She still cares,' I said. 'She asked me to tell you. Like you, I thought she was playing with you to begin with, but I was wrong. She believes in the Diggers, passionately, perhaps more than any of you.'

'I don't want to talk about it,' he said. 'It's finished.' He stooped to pick up his spade, smashed it into the only standing wall of the house.

Stones and lath tumbled and fell.

'Come away now.' I went around him to look into his face. His expression was angry, but his eyes were pools of pain. I put a hand on his shoulder, but he shrugged away from me. I brought out the letter. 'I have something to show you.'

'I don't want to read it.'

'No. It's not from her. It's from Grice. It's for Captain Wentworth at the Green Man. We must tell Father what's in it. I have to take a reply or I would have thrown it into a ditch.'

He gave it a cursory glance. 'It's sealed.' He was still sulking.

'I know, I brought a seal so we can re-seal it. It's her lady... I mean, I hope Captain Wentworth won't notice the seal's not Mr Grice's.'

When he hesitated I said, 'I'll open it then.'

He put the spade down then and held out his hand for the letter. 'Have you a flame?'

We sat on a wall and I brought out my flint. We used a burning stick to soften the wax enough to open it. Ralph puzzled over the words, mouthing them to himself.

'What does it say?' I asked him, leaning over his shoulder.

'Grice's telling him that the King's already on his way to Worcester.' He turned to face me so I could see his lips. 'And he's telling Wentworth that a Lady Eleanor Prescott will be travelling through here on her way to her brother's wedding next Thursday night. Her family's for the King.'

'What does it mean?'

'Grice is telling him it's a cover. There's no wedding at all. It's a device for bringing Royalist gold to the King.'

'So I was right. He's not to be trusted. He's giving away Royalist secrets. The turncoat. Let me look!'

He kept it away from my eager gaze and carried on reading;

'*Thank you for your reply to my message about Lady Prescott. You are right, we must stop her getting the gold to the King – he'll buy arms and mercenaries to shore up the city*', he says.

'*If William Chaplin must intercept her then I could lend support. Despite my injury, I'm not a bad shot...*'

Father's name! I snatched the paper from him. 'Let me see.'

'Careful!'

I scanned the words, picking out what I could. 'Grice is asking Wentworth to meet him at the Manor. It looks like Grice and Wentworth must have been writing to each other for some time. What's more, Grice has changed sides.'

Ralph looked up at me. 'Good for him. Maybe he's seen sense. He's right though. If we don't stop them buying more mercenaries, Parliament will have a heavy fight on their hands.'

I shook my head. 'Be careful – I would not trust Grice. I hate him. If he can blow one way with the wind, he can blow the other. Grice is stealing my mistress's lands, making her sign away her estate. She cannot refuse - he put a pistol to her throat. I saw him with my own eyes.'

Ralph turned to look at me, a stunned expression on his face. He opened his mouth as if he would say something, but then he stood and walked away. Put his face in his hands.

'Ralph,' I called after him.

He was hugging himself as if to hold himself together.

'Bloody war. How did we get to this? Englishman fighting Englishman? The end can't come soon enough.'

'What will you do?'

'You mean about Grice? Nothing. He's on our side.' It was a moment before he came and sat back beside me. 'But I'll talk to Father about Wentworth and this Lady Prescott,' he said. 'Father's not as quick as he was, and I'm the better rider, so I'm sure he can persuade Wentworth to let me go. If there could be trouble - and if as you say, Grice is not to be trusted, then one man stands much more chance of riding away.'

'Be careful though, we don't want them to know we opened the letter, or I'll be in awful trouble.'

'Do you think I'm a fool? Here, give the letter back to me and let's seal it up again.'

I held it as though it might bite me, but Ralph melted a new blob of wax onto it and I pressed Lady Katherine's seal into the hot wax. Ralph stared at it. 'That's the Fanshawe seal,' he said.

'Yes, the three fleurs-de-lis.'

'Is it hers?'

'Yes.' The atmosphere turned heavy. I put my hand on his sleeve, 'Have a heart, Ralph. Grice is dangerous. I fear for my mistress.'

'I don't care if they all rot.'

I knew that was not true, that it was just angry words, but he wasn't ready to listen to me. I tucked the letter back inside my bodice and mounted my pony.

I brought the short reply from Captain Wentworth's servant back to Grice and he was none the wiser. As I passed my mistress's room I saw Rigg and Pitman just coming out. Pitman tucked something hurriedly into his jerkin and exchanged a warning look with Rigg.

What were they up to? There was no time to think because I had to return milady's seal. I slipped into the study and eased open the drawer of the writing desk but just as I reached inside, a hand came onto my shoulder.

I almost shot up out of my shoes and dropped the seal where it rolled to rest at my mistress's feet.

'What are you doing?' Lady Katherine pulled me round.

'Nothing,' I said, unsure whether to address her as my mistress.

'That's my seal. What are you doing with it?'

I shook my head.

'Tell me.' She looked into my eyes, 'please.'

She had asked humbly. I weighed it up. We had both threatened each other enough. She hated Grice as much as I did. I decided to tell her the truth. 'I opened one of Grice's letters. To Captain Wentworth at the Green Man.'

'What did it say? Show me.' She was curious now, her anger less.

'I can't. I delivered it.' I told her of Lady Prescott and the smuggled Royalist gold. 'The gold will buy mercenaries. The men are tired, worn out with so much toil and fighting and so little progress. Ralph says both sides are desperate for more men, even if they have to pay for their loyalty. And everyone wants and end to it.'

Lady Katherine picked up the seal and paced up and down, her brow creased as she thought. 'So whoever gets the gold gets an advantage. If the King loses then my husband will be exiled or executed. My house will go to Grice or to Cromwell and I'll be without a roof over my head. But if the King wins then my husband will return and I will have to endure my step-father and his beatings.' She paused, shook her head sadly. 'In my position, which side would you choose?'

I could not answer. A pang of compassion made me twist the corner of my apron in my hands. Lady Katherine put the seal in the drawer and closed it gently but firmly. 'You will not touch my seal again. Do you understand?'

I pulled on a lock of hair that had escaped my cap and looked at the floor.

My mistress came towards me and touched my arm. 'Any more news from Ralph?' she asked me. 'Did he mention me when you saw him?' She was tentative, entreating.

'He's still angry.'

'Not anything? Didn't he say anything about me at all?'

I shook my head. She continued to walk up and down, up and down. Finally she stopped dead.

'I'm going to run away and join the Diggers. I shall persuade Ralph if it's the last thing I do. He's got to believe I care for him. I think of him all the time. It gives me such a pain, right here.' She pressed her hand to her chest. 'He's all I have. Please, Abi, you've got to help me talk to him.'

She used my name. My name on her lips squeezed my heart. I shook my head. 'I can't. I'm sorry. He's given it up. They've all gone home. He's joining my father in the army.'

'Given up the Diggers?'

'There's nobody left on the Common now. The Diggers have gone, gone to fight for Parliament.'

She sat down then heavily onto a chair, as if someone had pushed her over. Her skirts sank down after her like a sigh. 'Then I will have no future after all.'

It was a moment before she gathered herself together. A long moment where I stared awkwardly at my feet. When I saw the tips of her shiny boots disappear under her skirts I looked up. She had drawn herself up ram-rod straight and wiped her face of all emotion. 'You may go,' she said.

'I'm sorry.' My hand lifted towards her and fell back.

'Just go.'

CHAPTER SEVENTEEN

Jacob Mallinson

'Your brother's been arrested,' Mistress Binch said to me. 'This morning. The man who brought the milk said he saw him being brought down off the common with hand-irons on his wrists. Put up a right fight too, from all accounts. Poor John Soper ended up with a missing tooth. I never would have thought that of your brother, he seemed such a nice friendly lad.'

I begged Mistress Binch to let me have an hour to go home, and took Pepper and galloped as fast as I could to our cottage. Something was in the air, I could tell by the fact that people had their shutters closed even though it was daytime, and that there were no farm implements lying in the fields – no rakes, no scythes, and the corn was uncut in the fields. I could almost smell the war coming closer.

Even before I got to our house I could see the flashing tips of pikes - men performing drill up and down the road with my father at the head of the row. He saw me pass but did not acknowledge me. He was intent on his training. I shuddered at the thought that these weapons were designed to pierce the soft stomachs of other Englishmen and their horses.

When I got inside the house it was to find Mother with all her recipe books out straining herbs through muslin to make bottled remedies for the winter. William was strapped to her back with a cloth whilst she worked, and he was sleeping. Martha was knitting again. 'Look Abi, a hat,' she said.

I admired it with a smile, it was more dropped stitches than anything else. But like all children she had to learn.

'I thought you'd come,' Mother said. 'Poor Ralph. The first I heard of it was when a message came asking for bail. What went on? Did you see it? They said he was at the Manor.'

'He hit a servant. Where've they taken him?'

'The stupid dolt.' Mother put her strainer down. 'What was he thinking of?'

'He came to see me.' That at least was true. 'What do you think will happen to him?'

'They'll keep him there in the holding cell at the Constable's until the Quarter Assizes. Then he'll be tried, I suppose.' She sighed. 'And then Lord knows; the Fanshawes have never been known for their clemency. Your father's been down there this morning to try to get him out, but we've not enough ready money to bail him. Your father was counting on Ralph too, to go with him up to Wigan and then to Worcester for the last push against the King. It's an unholy mess, that's what it is. What on earth was Ralph thinking?' Most of this seemed to be talking to herself, but I read it well enough.

I skirted her question. 'I know the constable's son, Jacob. He's a friend of Ralph's. I'll go and talk to him, maybe he'll put in a word for him, be able to do something.'

'Do that. Heaven knows, I've no real wish for Ralph to join the army, but I'd rather that, than him lying useless in that cell. You know what he's like, he'll fall into a depression if he has to stay there any length of time.'

I picked up a stone jar from the table, weighed it in my hands.

'What's wrong?' Mother paused and looked up at my troubled face.

'Nothing.'

Mother sat down on the stool and untied William to lay him in the crib. 'If it isn't one thing, it's another. Tell me,' she said. 'Is it that cook? If it is I'll —'

'No. Not Mistress Binch, she's all right. We've got used to each other. There's really nothing to tell. They are closing up the house that's all.' As I said it a lump came to my throat and I realised I really did care. That I could not imagine a life with no Markyate Manor, no Lady Katherine.

'Oh Abi. I'm sorry.'

I stood to leave because I was scared I'd show my feelings, and crying blocked my eyes and took me back into a silent world cut off from everyone else.

Mother patted my arm, 'I'll ask in the village,' she said, 'tell folks you'll be looking. There'll be a place for a girl as clever as you, I know there will, now you've shown you're a good worker, and they'll give you a proper reference, won't they?'

I nodded, and evaded her hug. I didn't want to be mothered, I wanted to show her I didn't need her, didn't need help. Besides, I really didn't want to work for anyone else. Markyate Manor and Lady Katherine had crept up on me.

'I'll be off to Jacob's then,' I said.

'Go careful on that road,' she said, but I shrugged off her embrace.

Outside, I passed Father and the others still training with their pikes - lunge and thrust, retreat, lunge and thrust. Sweat dewed dark on the back of their jerkins but I did not stop. I mounted Pepper and headed for Jacob's tithe cottage.

He wasn't in when I knocked, but I went round the back and he was there hoeing a small vegetable patch. A trug basket on the wall was stuffed with vegetables – sprouts, cabbage, peas and beans, kale and a bowl of raspberries from the raspberry canes. Jacob stood up at my approach.

'That's a good harvest,' I said.

I was shy so it made me red-faced to watch his lips. 'I'm getting it out of the garden,' he said. 'There's rumours troops will pass along this road, and I don't want to be giving it away.' He smiled.

'Can I help?'

'You can help me bring it inside and wash it if you like.' His manner was easy, but I was all fingers and thumbs as I lifted up the basket and followed him to the house. 'You sit there,' he said, 'and I'll fetch water.'

I sat on one of the stools by the fireplace feeling nervous to be sitting all alone in a young man's house. For months I'd dreamt of being alone with Jacob Mallinson, but now the moment had come I was scared. I felt like my hands were too big, twining themselves in my lap. And I did not know what Jacob might think about Ralph hitting someone, or about me asking him a favour.

The room was barely furnished but tidy. A pierced cupboard for his larder was set into the wall. Looking up I saw daylight through the thatch where some of it was blown away and wondered if he would get it fixed before winter.

He'd come in as I looked up, saw what I was staring at. 'I'll get round to it eventually,' he said, 'now we're not building on the common. The Fanshawes will never fix it, even though I'm their tenant.'

'I've come to see you about that,' I said. 'Well, about Ralph, really.'

He waited, pulled out another stool from behind the table.

'He hit one of the servants up at the Manor and now he's locked up and I wondered if you could, I mean...' After the gush of words I faltered.

Jacob leaned towards me, eyes full of curiosity, 'Was it really Lady Katherine Fanshawe – the Kate that came to our meetings?'

'Yes. That's what started it.'

He thumped the table with his fist, delighted. 'Ha! I told Ralph it was her, when we saw her on the road, but he denied it, said I was talking nonsense. But I could tell he was rattled by the way he hared off after you, and I knew as soon as he did there'd be trouble. He always was a bit quick-fisted, Ralph. You'll be wanting me to speak to my father, I suppose.'

'Would you?'

'I could, but it would probably do more harm than good. Father's dead set against the Diggers and I can't see him wanting to let Ralph out, knowing he's the leader. He didn't like it when I came home all cut up from the Common. He'll doubtless think it best Ralph stays where he is. And if I try to persuade him it will only make him dig in his heels deeper. He thinks Ralph's a bad influence.'

'But I can't leave him there. It's months until the Assizes. And we've no money to bail him.'

'What about Lady Katherine? She seemed sweet enough on Ralph. Maybe she could help. God's truth, I never guessed who she was. And Ralph thinking she was the girl for him all this time and never even having an inkling!'

'She really believed in the Diggers.'

Jacob raised his eyebrows. 'I can't believe that's true. We wanted to build a better life, one where working folk weren't so hand-to-mouth. Why would she need that? She's already wealthy enough.'

'Her family might be rich, but they're all monsters. I think she was lonely. She wanted a little companionship, to be with people like us, young people with ideals she believes in. And she loves Ralph. She hasn't said so, but I know she does.'

He looked up at me, and his eyes caught mine. Suddenly I was aware of us alone here in the room, the closeness of him, where I could almost touch him. He held my gaze, leaned closer in. I could not tear my eyes from his. A spark flew between us.

All at once, looking at his lips seemed brazen, far too intimate.

'And here was I, thinking you'd come to see me,' he said.

I burned hot, unsure how to reply. I stood up and made a fuss of tucking my neckerchief into my bodice and tidying my hair under its cap. 'I'll be going then, I'll go and see if I can visit Ralph.'

'Hey, you're running away,' he said, smiling, reaching out a hand to stay me.

'I'm not,' I said crossly, shooting backwards out of the door, 'it's just I've got things to do.' But I felt all out of kilter, as if someone had knocked me over and I wasn't quite steady on my feet. I hurried to mount my pony, but he held its bridle for me with a calm hand.

'You're a strange one,' he said. 'But you're very pretty, Abigail Chaplin, did you know that?'

But perhaps I misheard.

CHAPTER EIGHTEEN

Ladybird, Ladybird

Lady Katherine did not send for me again that night. I felt bad about having to tell her Ralph had given up the Diggers. She weighed on my mind. I wanted to give her some good news, so I tried again to get into Grice's room to fetch out his letters. Rigg almost caught me and I had to whip out a kerchief and pretend I was dusting. He made a lunge for me, but I dodged under his arm, out of his way.

I felt at a loss, unsure what to do with no mistress to see to, so when I had finished my chores I went to my own garret. I could not sleep for worrying about Ralph, stuck in that cell. And Jacob hadn't seemed optimistic about sweet-talking his father to get him out.

Jacob. I hoped he did not think me too forward, arriving like that on his threshold. He'd understand that it was only for Ralph, wouldn't he? I remembered the feeling of sitting opposite him at his table, and felt myself blush all over again. He was so tall, and he made me feel so shivery inside.

Was this love? I didn't know.

Did Lady Katherine feel like this about my brother? I was pondering this when all of a sudden the thought struck me. Lady Katherine's hoard of coin. It would be enough to get Ralph out.

Five minutes later I had wheedled my way past Pitman and I was in my mistress's chamber. She was already dressed in her nightclothes, her hair tumbling about her shoulders.

'Ralph's in gaol. I wanted to tell you, but couldn't get near you without Grice or his men hearing.'

Her eyebrows shot up, her face fell. 'Grice?'

'Yes. He had him arrested for blacking the servant's eye. They want five pounds to buy his freedom.'

'In God's name! Why did you not tell me before? Can nothing be done?'

'My wages won't cover that, even if Grice saw fit to pay me, which so far he never has,' She began to speak but I swept on, 'You've got to get Ralph out.'

'Me? I can't –'

'You've got money, coins, I know you have,' I blurted.

'No, I have nothing. I wish I had.'

'What about under there?' I pointed at the loose floorboard.

'You…?' She put her hand to her forehead. 'Wait. Let me think.'

But I would not wait, I got down on my knees and pulled at the loose board. 'There's enough – ' The board came away. I was staring at a black empty hole.

I looked up at her. 'Where is it?'

'I tried to tell you. I don't have it. It's gone. When it went missing, I thought you'd taken it.'

'Me? Why would I?' I was outraged.

'Keep your voice down, they'll hear you. It's not so foolish. After all you're the one that knows about it, are you not? '

'Yes, but I'd never steal from you.' I could barely blurt out the words. 'I don't know how you can think that.' I turned away in a sulk, but then swung round to fire back, 'you're the one that's a thief, not I.'

She crushed a handful of her skirt in her fist, screwed it tight. Her face showed she was thinking, weighing it up. She sighed and let the bunched fabric drop. 'You're right,' she said. 'At first I just wanted to scare Lady Ann - get back what she had taken. But afterwards it was such a comfort knowing I had something put away, that I could do something. If I ever needed to run away, I mean. I didn't know how much longer I could bear it; the beatings when Sir Simon and Thomas were home.' Her green eyes looked candidly into mine, 'It was after I'd dressed as a servant girl. I realised, if I could disguise myself as one thing, why not another?'

I gasped in protest. 'That's right, try to blame it on me.'

She managed a smile. 'No, I'm not, I swear. And then my pouch was stolen, and I hadn't the heart to do it again. Not after meeting the Diggers. I kept thinking of what Ralph and Jacob would think. They were so upright and honest, not like my husband and his stepfather'

'They're swine. Not gentlemen, despite their titles,' I said. 'But even so, I couldn't have done it, ridden out like that in the dark.'

She sat on the bed. 'The first time I nearly turned back. But I was mad with anger too, at the way Lady Ann had just taken my belongings as if it was her right. The anger fired my courage. When I put my pistol through the coach window and saw the fear on Lady Ann's face, I almost laughed. I'd been scared of the Fanshawes so often. Now the boot was on the other foot for a change. It made me bold. But I vowed to myself I'd never steal again, that I'd try to be Kate, the girl Ralph was so proud to know.'

I pulled at a thread that dangled from my apron. I was thinking. If it wasn't me who took the pouch, it had to be someone else. I remembered the shifty expression on Rigg's face, and how Pitman had bundled something away into his pocket.

'I think it was Grice's servants who stole it. I saw Rigg come out of your room, looking like he'd done something he shouldn't.'

She sighed, 'It's all right. I believe you. I know it wasn't you.'

'I'm telling you, it was Rigg and Pitman,' I insisted.

'It makes no difference. It's gone now anyway, and we can't exactly report it missing, can we?' She knelt to put the floorboard back in its place. A few moments later she asked me, 'Can nothing be done for Ralph?'

'Not unless you can persuade Grice to drop the charges.'

'I'll try,' she said. But we both knew that was hopeless.

At dawn I was woken by Mistress Binch shaking me. I was in the middle of a dream where I was stuck in a sinking ship and was slowly drowning. It took me a few moments to realise that she was telling me my sister Elizabeth was downstairs in the kitchen.

When I got down, Elizabeth was pacing the flagstones, pink-cheeked but tight-lipped with fury. She fired words at me like arrows.

'You've to do something,' she said. 'Talk to Lady Katherine, tell them she can stay.'

I blinked, shook my head, not knowing what she meant, not sure I'd understood.

'What have you done?' Elizabeth said, 'You've been dismissed, haven't you?'

'No! I don't know what you're talking about. Talk slowly, I can't understand that gabble.'

From the corner of my eye I saw Mistress Binch, her eyes open wide, goggling at our conversation.

'It's Mother. Your precious Lady Katherine has thrown her out. No notice given, nothing. Just came yesterday afternoon and said to be out by noon.'

'Who came? What are you talking about?'

'Grice! And one of his flunkies. She's frantic. Where will she go?'

I backed away to try and find a little space. 'I don't know anything about it, it's nothing to do with me. It's Ralph. He hit one of Grice's men.'

'Soon as I heard it was at the Manor, I knew you had something to do with it. You just can't keep out of trouble, can you?'

I didn't want to listen, 'What about Father? Can't he help?'

Elizabeth came closer until I was backed up against the kitchen wall. 'He's useless. He says he hasn't got the time for it all now with the King's troops bearing down on us. All he thinks about is the fighting. He says Mother's to go to his sister's, but you know she won't. She hates Aunt Agnes. She say's she'd rather join Ralph and his crazy Diggers. Except Ralph's in gaol, isn't he, thanks to you.' She poked a finger into my chest. 'I don't know what's been going on here, but I know it's your doing, all this trouble. Just like last time.'

The barb hit home as she knew it would.

It was true, I'd brought them all nothing but trouble. My sister always had the power to make me feel small. Tears sprang to my eyes.

Elizabeth's mouth turned down in disgust. 'Crying's no use. You've to talk to Grice, beg him to reconsider. Tell him she's nowhere to go.'

'Now just a minute, young lady,' Mistress Binch inserted her skinny frame between us. Elizabeth tried to step to one side, but Mistress Binch squared up to Elizabeth and looked her full in the face. 'You can't come in here upsetting everyone like that. Whatever's gone on at home, it can't be Abigail's fault. She's been right here working with me. Now if you can't keep your tongue, you'd better get out of my kitchen.'

She looked so fierce that Elizabeth was momentarily speechless. I saw my sister's mouth open and close in a stutter before she shouted at me, 'You'd better do something. Unless you want Mother and the two little ones sleeping rough. She knows it's you, doesn't she? That Ralph going to gaol and all this is your fault, but she always says we've to make allowances. Allowances. Nobody ever made any allowances for me. I had to –'

'Out.' Mistress Binch pushed her through the open door and closed it firmly behind her.

When Mistress Binch turned to me my eyes were blurred so I couldn't make out her words, but she took hold of me in a bony embrace and gave me a rag to blow my nose. I struggled out of her grip and managed to say, 'Beg pardon, mistress.'

Her face had a soft look about it. 'I can manage, if you want to go and talk to Mr Grice. Tell you what, I'll give you some of my hot lardy cakes. That will sweeten him up a bit.'

I wiped my face whilst she put two cakes on the griddle. When she handed them over she said, 'He's turned bitter, these last months, Mr Grice. He never used to be like that. He roused up a right rabble against those poor folks on the Common, them that were meeting in our old barn. I wished I'd never told him. They went for them like savages with picks and spades. Now this. Turning people out of their homes, it's sinful. You get along now, see what you can do for your poor Ma.'

I took the platter to the study but Mr Grice was not there, and there was no sign of Lady Katherine. Perhaps he was in his room. I went up and knocked, pushing it open a fraction as I always did to see if he was in.

The room was empty. One of the letters that should have gone to Lady Katherine lay opened on the bed. I recognised Thomas's handwriting. I glanced over my shoulder before putting down the plate and leaning over to read it. It was folded over so I could not read all of it, but I made out a few sentences,

'so Lady Ann's manservant will check all is well with you until we can find a new overseer. Grice was insolent to my stepfather last time they met and he has been told

*to look for employment elsewhere. I am afraid that de-
spite his long service with the family, we simply cannot
keep him on...'*

A sixth sense alerted me to something behind me and
I snatched up the plate. Grice glared at me and I took an
involuntary step away.

'What are you doing?'

'I've brought you some hot lardy cakes,' I said, act-
ing simple.

'No. I didn't ask for any. They must be for Lady
Katherine.' He waved me away. 'Stupid girl,' I saw him
mutter.

His look told me he wasn't going to listen, but I
ploughed on regardless. 'Excuse me Sir, but about my
mother...' I planted my feet firmly, hoped I didn't look
as scared as I felt. 'You gave her notice. Won't you think
again, Sir?'

'Do you dare to question what I do? I told you. Unruly tenants won't be tolerated. Get back to your mistress.'

'But I –'

He lunged towards the door with his arm raised as if
he would strike me. I closed the door in his face with my
free hand and the lardy cakes shot off the plate and onto
the floor.

As I was picking them up Mr Grice came out of his
room and almost tripped over me. I cringed away from

him as I saw a stream of expletives come from his mouth.

It was only then that the words of Thomas's letter sunk in. Grice had been dismissed. He shouldn't be here giving me orders at all.

I told Mistress Binch what I had read, but I could see she didn't want to believe me.

'You must be mistaken,' she kept saying. 'He wouldn't do that – come here and take charge. Not if he's no right to. And Sir Simon wouldn't give him notice – he's worked for them forever.' Her face was troubled, uncertain.

'He's never given me a single penny in wages,' I said.

We stared at each other a moment.

'Nor me, neither. Not for the last few months.'

'And he won't relent - about my mother, I mean.'

Mistress Binch dried her hands. 'Never mind the polishing today, you'd best get on home. See if you can help your Ma. I'll manage. I need time to think.'

When I got to our cottage, the door was planked and nailed shut. The lace had gone from the front window, so it stared at me like a blank eye. It gave me an ache in my stomach when I pressed my nose to the window and saw only an empty room.

Neighbours told me my family were saying at the smith's house for the night.

When I went there I saw the handcart outside with my father's fireside chair loaded on it, and the crib, and the rest of our possessions all on view for everyone to see on the street. It was shaming, that we owned so little. Through the window I saw my mother sitting at their kitchen table feeding William. She looked exhausted.

I could not bear to go in. To see her sad face, and to know it was all my fault again. Elizabeth was right. If I hadn't lent Lady Katherine my clothes then Ralph wouldn't have fallen for Kate and then he wouldn't have hit Pitman and none of this would have happened. I turned away from the window and walked away in the gathering dusk.

When I first came to the Manor, I'd come to try and make it right – to put the past behind me and make amends to Mother for what I'd done all those years before. But all I'd done now was make it worse.

It had been an evening just like this one, warm and brooding, with the corn dry as tinder, that I'd made the spell. Was it only five years ago? It seemed so much longer. I stopped to catch my breath and leaned over the kissing gate. I remembered it as if it was yesterday.

'My sampler's better than yours,' Elizabeth had said.

She was right of course, because she was older and quicker, and I knew Mistress Maple, our governess, would be sure to give the prize - the box of confits - to her. I was a slow stitcher, but neat, and so I thought if only Elizabeth could be ill for a few days, then I would be able to catch up.

Mother's recipe books had some spells at the back too, written there by a well-meaning neighbour and these were my favourite reading. I remembered the writing so well, the faded spidery hand, the lists of unlikely ingredients. The feeling that you could hold a sprinkle of magic right there in your hand. And one recipe in particular had stuck in my memory - the title at the top of the page – *'to cure sicknesse of the stomache, or to give it.'*

'To give it.' That set me thinking. The recipe was easy, only common herbs such as we already had in our well-stocked larder. The hardest part would be to go into Elizabeth's room at night. She hated me going in her room, probably because she feared I might find the little tweezers she used to pluck her brows into a bow-shape, the tint of madder she used for her lips.

On the night I did it, I could hear my family beneath me, voices and laughter, my mother chuckling at a joke my father made. It was the last time I heard that sound. For as I was grinding my spirit of buckthorn, my wild garlic, the bulb of wormwood together in the pestle, thinking it was all a great game, I had taken no heed of the candle I had left burning on the window ledge. The window was open to give a little air and the flame flailed and flickered. I did not see the danger, even then.

I waited until the whole house was sleeping and I could hear father's snores before I went to Elizabeth's chamber. In those days she had her own small room in the eaves – a room she guarded jealously from the prying eyes of her little sister. All I had to do was to place the foul-smelling bundle on Elizabeth's stomach as she slept and remove it before she woke. I remember sneaking across the landing, a delicious giggly feeling inside. I did not know then that casting spells was wicked.

Next thing I knew, the stairwell was full of smoke and the servants running hither and thither with brooms and buckets. Father's shouts and mother's screams as Father tried to fight his way into my chamber, thinking I was still asleep in there. The fire had taken hold already and orange flames and heat pushed him back. When I appeared in the hall, still clutching mother's recipe book, he cried, 'God be praised!' and he hugged me until I was breathless before thrusting me coughing into the night.

The neighbours were too slow with their fire buckets, and what with dealing with Martha and William, Mother could not help. Elizabeth stood by me in her nightdress, a damp green stain over her stomach, and just stared.

Smoke belched from the door. Windows cracked and shattered. The thatch of the roof caved in, showering us with glowing sparks, as the house creaked and groaned under the roar of the fire. We threw on what water we could, beat at it with brooms, but it only raged harder.

The wind had caught the fire between its teeth and would not let it go.

Nobody ever asked if I had left a candle burning, but all knew I had. Elizabeth would say things like, 'it started in Abigail's room,' when people asked.

The curtain must have blown across the flame. I imagined the edge of the fabric tickling the flame until it lapped the hem. The slow grasping of fiery fingers moving up the curtain until the whole thing was ablaze. I shuddered. Even now, the thought was enough to make me squeeze my eyes tight shut, as if that could shut out the memories and the awful hollow pain of grief.

And Elizabeth's bitterness and blame followed me everywhere I went.

'Everything's ruined,' Elizabeth said. 'We've nothing left. I'll have no dowry. Who will want to marry me now?'

As I walked back to the Manor I pondered on these dark thoughts. Of how we had to move to the tithe cottage – a place so damp and unwelcoming when we arrived that Mother wept. And we were all ill that winter. The messels raged through the row of tithe cottages. At the end of it, all the other children stood up again the same as before.

But not me. For me the world had closed its mouth. I knew why – it was punishment for what I'd done.

When I got back to the Manor, it was full dusk and the bats were doing their flit from barn to chimney. At night in bed I wished I could turn back time and worried about how to help Mother and Ralph. That interloper Grice had not yet paid me a farthing.

And I thought of Lady Katherine facing a future with the odious Sir Simon and his cowardly son, if they ever came back, not to mention Mr Grice. Whatever the future held for me, it could not be worse than it would be for Lady Katherine – stuck here with Mr Grice with his festering leg and bad breath. At least if the worst came to the worst, I could leave. She did not have that choice.

I realised there was not another soul who cared for her, only us. I remembered Ralph's animated face whenever he talked of Kate. For the first time I wished that Lady Katherine really was Kate, and that she could be a part of my family. But I did not dare break it to my mistress that Mr Grice should not be here at all, that he had been dismissed. I had not forgotten his threat with the pistol. I would have to persuade someone to help us.

CHAPTER NINETEEN

A Death

The next morning I was about to go up to Lady Katherine, but Grice would not let me go to my mistress. Instead he told her to keep to her chambers. Rigg and Pitman were to keep her company. But when I glanced up the stairs I saw them lounging outside her door. She was trapped indoors again. Meanwhile I was to sweep the rugs in the yellow chamber and the study, polish the grates and air the rooms for Grice was expecting a visit from Captain Wentworth.

I dare not disobey, but scratched at the rugs with the broom until I ran with sweat. I wanted to tell my mistress about how Grice should not be here, and taking orders from him now made me resentful. It took me all morning to do the tasks I was given, and then Grice demanded that I dress his wound again and polish his specially-made boots. He gave me instructions as to my duties when Wentworth came – opening the door, fetching refreshments, serving at table.

When I was done, I tried to get in to see my mistress again but was sent away by Pitman. Captain Wentworth arrived at about four o'clock, cantering up on his big bay horse. Mr Grice nodded at me to fetch cakes and ale.

'If it's for Captain Wentworth, I'm not giving my food to that pig.' Mistress Binch stood before the door waving her skinny arms and shouting like a fishwife. I shuffled from foot to foot uncertain what to do but finally I nipped past her for the jug and ale on a tray, but left the cakes on the plates.

The men were seated in the reading room on two leather upholstered chairs.

'There seems to be some sort of disturbance below,' said the Captain.

'I didn't hear anything,' Grice said.

The Captain smiled with supercilious amusement, and I detected a flicker of discord between the two men.

I had barely set out the tankards when the door flung open. Mistress Binch burst over the threshold, her face set for a storm.

'Mistress Binch,' Grice said, before she could speak. 'The Captain will be staying for dinner. Lady Katherine is to –'

'No.' Mistress Binch took a deep breath so her scrawny chest puffed out like a pigeon. 'I'm not staying another minute. I don't know what's come over you, but I'd rather try my luck at Lady Ann's. At least she keeps an honest household.' Grice was about to speak but she rode over his words. 'Look at you! Sir Simon would flay you alive if he could see you now, doling out ale to Cromwell's pigs.'

'Get out.' Grice had found his tongue.

But Mistress Binch was not done. She pointed at him, her face tight with rage. 'I know what you are. You shouldn't even be here, eating his food and quaffing his ale. He sacked you, and with good reason. Traitors, the lot of you, to the King's good name. I spit on you.' And she hawked a gobbet of spit towards Grice's boots.

Mistress Binch was out of the door before Grice could even lift a hand. His face flushed beetroot. He yelled for his servants. Captain Wentworth suppressed a superior smile as Grice hobbled into the hall, too slow to catch her.

I was rigid, tied to the spot. Grice would know I had read his letter. From the window I could see Mistress Binch striding determinedly down the path. A small thin figure, empty-handed, her apron ties flapping, her back stiff as a wall as if to put us behind her. She was walking away from us with no reference and not a single possession. Half of me wanted to chase after her shouting, 'wait for me!' But loyalty to Lady Katherine was stronger and I stayed put.

Grice returned and made an attempt at humour. 'Servants! You can never trust them, can you? Always one thing or another.' I pressed my lips together and tried not to let his insult rankle. Grice's face was one that was unused to smiling and it soon fell back into its disgruntled frown. 'I'll have her charged,' he said.

'Don't mind on my account. Let her go,' Wentworth said lazily. 'Plenty more fish in the sea. Or cooks, should I say.' He turned to me, 'Can you cook?'

I opened my mouth to reply but Grice said, 'Her? No. She can't do much. She's deaf as a tree-trunk and twice as stupid ...' He paused, gave me a penetrating look. He came over to me, grabbed me by the chin, his cold eyes searched mine.

'Can you read?' he asked.

I forced myself to shake my head dumbly.

He tightened the grip on my throat, but I continued to look blankly at him. 'Are you as stupid as you look, Abigail Chaplin?' I did not react. He pushed me away from him, and I bobbed a curtsey as if it pleased me. 'Idiot girl,' he said.

Captain Wentworth glanced at me as if I were of little interest.

'What are you gawping at, fetch us ale.' Grice said to me.

By the time I came back with the jug they were sitting talking about Lady Prescott and the gold. Captain Wentworth had big flabby lips under his ginger moustache. They were easy to read.

'Shame for it all to go on mercenaries,' Wentworth said. 'Especially as I haven't been paid my dues for nigh on six months.'

'What are you saying?' Grice's eyes grew sharper.

Wentworth whispered, 'We could split it. Half to the army, half to us.'

I poured the ale, and Grice tapped his fingers on the table. I could see he did not trust Wentworth.

Wentworth went on, 'Come on, man. What's to stop us? Nobody else knows about it. In fact, if it didn't get there at all, who'd be the wiser?'

I could not stay because I had served the ale and to be there longer would have looked strange. And I needed to think. I could not believe Mistress Binch had really gone. I put my eye to the keyhole to see if I could read their conversation. When they were side-on against the window like that, it was not too hard.

'Our troops are already at St Alban's,' Wentworth said, 'they're lusting for blood and to finish this war. God help any Royalist in their way.'

'When will they get here?' Grice said.

'In the early hours of the morning, I guess.'

I was uncertain I had made it out correctly and I couldn't see more because Grice stood up, and his back came between my spyhole and Wentworth. After a few moments I crept away. But if I had got it right, Cromwell's men were coming, they would be men intent on blood and plunder, and the mere thought turned me cold.

When I went to get milk from the churn, I saw Lady Katherine's face, pale at the window like a moth to the light. She had been sad since Ralph had rejected her. It gave me a twinge of pain to see her like that, so unlike the imperious mistress I first met.

I did my best in the kitchen but there was no time to cook the ingredients on the table, so I could only provide left-over potage and bread. It was a soulless, empty place without Mistress Binch. If it wasn't for the fact I was owed more than two month's wages, I would be tempted to leave myself. But I could not. I could not leave Lady Katherine all alone.

Battle was drawing closer, I could feel it. A stillness in the air, a foreboding that made my spine shiver and the blood race widdershins round my body. And I could not leave now in any case, I had nowhere to go. Besides, despite her treatment of me, Lady Katherine had grown in my affection in a way I had not expected. God knows, I had not thought to feel any loyalty to her, but somehow I did.

While the men talked Grice instructed me to accompany Lady Katherine on an evening stroll in the grounds. Now I knew Grice was a liar, and not supposed to be in charge, he scared me. No doubt he and Wentworth were discussing strategies for the forthcoming battle against the King's Army. I could not believe they were fighting on the same side as my father, these sour-faced men.

Pitman watched us set off from beside the front door, with a musket by his side. There was nobody to help

Lady Katherine now, I realised. They were all her enemies.

As soon as we were clear of the house, I said, 'You've got to listen! Grice is a liar and a fake. Your husband does not even know he's here.' I told her about the letter.

'Are you sure? There's no mistake?' She looked as if a puff of wind might blow her over. She walked away from me past the rows of roses, sweet-scented in the evening air, looking in a daze towards the far horizon.

When she came back, I said, 'He threw my mother out of her cottage too, no notice or anything.'

'How dare he!' She paced up and down. 'What shall we do? The gall of the man! But I daren't try to get rid of him. You saw how he threatened me.'

'We'll have to pretend we don't know. Get word to someone. Write to your husband.' A pang of guilt. 'I'll make sure the letter goes, this time, I promise.'

'Pitman's staring at us, better stroll on,' she said, 'act like we're looking at the garden.' We picked a few roses and walked over onto the lawn, heading towards the long shadow of the big oak. The sun was low in the sky by now, barely over the horizon.

'I can't believe it,' she said, 'Grice cheating us all this time. He's sold the rugs from under our feet, the pewter from our table. Made me sign away the mill and the cottages, pretending it was all instructions from Sir Simon.' She put her hand over her mouth, a thought had just come. 'Oh my Lord. My husband and Sir Simon will kill me. They'll think I'm to blame. What am I to do?'

'I don't know. I'm sorry now that I didn't disobey Grice's orders sooner. But I never knew –'

'It's not your fault. We must think who to tell. The Fanshawes have not much support round here, I don't know if anyone will help us.' She paced away from me but then turned back, her face drawn with anguish. 'I wish I were Kate. I wish the Diggers were here with their advice. Ralph would know what to do, or Jacob.'

'They won't release him unless someone pays.' I told her about my visit to Jacob. 'And he'll be so frustrated, sitting there unable to do anything. Tonight was the night he was supposed to –'

The coach. I had a sudden intuition. The gold. It would be enough to get Ralph out.

'What is it?' My mistress had seen the thought cross my face.

'The Silent Highwayman. You could hold up Lady Prescott's coach.'

She looked at me blankly.

'Don't you remember? Grice is talking with Captain Wentworth about it right now. They're going to intercept her at the crossroads. Ralph had volunteered to take the gold with Wentworth, but he can't now he's in gaol, Grice is going instead. But what if the Silent Highwayman got there first, I mean you –'

'No.' She shook her head emphatically. 'I made a vow not to. There's trouble enough, and this is the King's gold, not just a few trinkets.'

'You're right. Sorry. It's a foolish idea. And it would be too dangerous. Wentworth was wanting Grice to help him, and then to share the spoils between them, but I fear Grice wants keep it for himself...' I stopped. She wasn't listening to me anymore.

Her darting eyes showed she was thinking. 'I think you could be right. It could work,' she said. 'Abi, I could go myself, fetch him out of gaol. Ralph couldn't be angry at me any more if I did this for him. After all, it's not just robbery is it? It's for Parliament – to help end the fighting. Ralph wanted to stop the gold reaching the King's Army.'

I wished I'd never suggested it. I was filled with doubt now, because I realised Wentworth and Grice would be out there, and who knows how many other armed troops.

But Lady Katherine was alight with enthusiasm. 'He'd see I am on his side! It's perfect. It would count for something with Ralph, I'm sure, if I'd helped the Parliament cause. Wouldn't it?'

'But you're a royalist.'

'I'm a Digger.'

'It will be too heavy for you to carry. Bits of coin and jewellery fit easily in a pocket, but that –'

'I can do it, I know I can.' She ran over to me, took hold of my hands. 'I can hide the rest of the gold somewhere and then Ralph can go back to collect it.' She saw I did not look convinced, and she squeezed my fingers. 'If Ralph believed in me, he might ask the Diggers to help us, persuade Jacob's father to arrest Grice.'

I shrugged. 'I don't know.' The idea suddenly seemed outlandish, mad.

'It's worth trying.'

'It would be risking your life.'

She walked to the hedge and stared at the house, at its windows reflecting back the pink-tinged sky. 'I have no life. Not one worth living.' When she turned, her whole demeanour had changed. The jut of her chin told me she would not let me dissuade her. 'At the old packhorse bridge,' she said. 'Before the crossroads. They'll have to slow there because it's so narrow. Coaches have to ford the stream.' She talked with her hands, curving shapes in the air to show bridge and water.

We looked at each other and my heart drummed hard in my chest.

My mistress went quiet then, and we strolled back towards the house. I wanted to shout at her, to tell her not to go, but I knew it would be no use. She never listened to anyone once her mind was made up. As we approached Pitman gestured angrily at us to go away and walk round the garden again. We walked silently arm in arm for another fifteen minutes, as the last of the sun winked over the horizon, both of us alone with our thoughts.

She stopped dead.

'What was that?' I asked. Something had startled her.

'Sorry,' she said, 'probably nothing. I'm jumpy as a hare.' She let go of my arm, and relaxed. 'Just a distant shot. Someone scaring crows, or after deer. There hasn't been much stag-hunting on our land since my stepfather went away, that's all.'

I did not care about farmers and their sport. 'It's tonight,' I said, 'that Lady Prescott is riding through.'

'I know. I could have wished for a better night, one with no moon. Tonight there will be a harvest moon, enough to see my shadow on the highway.'

'Are you sure you still want to go? Maybe there's another way.'

'We need some men on our side to help us drive out Grice. Ralph and his friends are the only men I trust. Besides, Lady Prescott is a brave soul,' said Lady Katherine. 'She risks her life for her King. If she can brave the highway at night, then so can I. Though I would not like to be in her place - not with Grice and Wentworth waiting like wolves in the dark. And now I must add to her troubles.'

I did not say anything, but wondered at her courage. Lady Prescott would be armed, or probably guarded, carrying a cargo like that. My mistress might never come back. If she failed, what then? My family would be homeless, my brother would languish in gaol, and I would be without a livelihood.

Lady Katherine took hold of my arm. Rigg was signalling that we could go back inside. Once inside the door I could smell the faint but unmistakeable tang of gunpowder. My mistress went to her room, but I lingered in the hall.

The smell bothered me. A shot had been fired inside, I was certain. The noise that Lady Katherine heard. I followed my nose into the main chamber. In there, the scent was more metallic, hotter. It wasn't just the smell of the wax candles or the wall sconces. I looked around for any sign of where the shot might have gone, but could see no marks anywhere on the wall.

A slight damp smear on the floor. I crouched to look more closely. Directly above, on the wall were tiny dark spots. A spatter like the pattern on a bird's egg. I picked up a candle and went closer. Blood.

Someone had been shot in here, and the mess wiped from the floor.

CHAPTER TWENTY

Highway Maid

G rice and his two men passed, silhouettes in front of the window. So the blood had to be Captain Wentworth's. I had not seen him leave. Maybe he was wounded somewhere. My head swam, but I hurried down to the kitchen, nauseous, clinging to the rope banister.

Wentworth's horse was not there. Another dribble of dark by the back gate and the slight snaking marks in the grass that showed something had been dragged that way. I stood by the gate and there was just enough light for me to see that the trail went in the direction of the river. Almost without thinking I followed it, sweating under my bodice with apprehension.

Captain Wentworth was face down in the water, caught in some low ash branches overhanging the flow. I knew he was dead because his back was split open like a rose and no more blood flowed from him. He was still but for the movement of his hair in the water.

I shivered, as if I too was under that knife-cold water. Then I turned and ran, fast as I could back to Markyate Manor. On the way I passed Captain Wentworth's horse wandering loose and aimless, reins and stirrups flapping.

Fear for Lady Katherine powered my legs. Mistress Binch had gone. My mistress was all alone. If Grice could do this, what else might he do?

When I reached the Manor I was breathless, but all seemed calm and orderly. I glanced in the study. Grice was his usual self, poring over maps of the countryside in the waning light of the window. His men lounged on Sir Simon's chairs as if they owned them, puffing on their pipes of tobacco.

Would you do that if you had shot a man? I began to wonder if I had imagined it.

Grice looked over his shoulder and caught me staring. His eyes sent a chill through me. 'Have you no work to do? Go and light the lights, make yourself useful in the kitchen.'

The kitchen was empty, there was nothing there for me now Mistress Binch had gone. Instead I took a candle and crept up the stairs to Grice's room. I needed to know everything. I was extra careful because I could not hear the noise I made. I hoped his door did not creak as I pushed it open. I needed to see the rest of his correspondence, anything to tell me I was right, that Grice had just killed Captain Wentworth. Even though Grice pretended to be a Parliament man himself now.

The room smelt of that strange sour smell that Grice
always had. His travelling trunks were open, as if he was
packing to go away. A long-nosed pistol lay on the bed
and I touched a forefinger to the muzzle. Was it my imagination, or was it warm? I pulled away. It made me
shiver to look at it.

A litter of papers lay on the small side table. I picked
through the pile, trying not to drip wax onto them. Nothing. Just bills of sale signed in Sir Simon's hand - or was
it Grice's hand, forging the Fanshawe name? Household
bills, receipts. I pulled open a drawer. An unfinished letter rested there. It was addressed to Sir Simon Fanshawe.
I bent over, pressed my skirts against my knees, held the
light close to see it better. I began to read.

*By the time you read this your son's house will be a
garrison for Parliament troops and your farms un-ten-
anted, your land and furniture sold. I served you and
your Royalist swine faithfully for twenty years and got
no thanks, only scorn. I am half a man now, thanks to
you. I curse the family of Fanshawe. But there will be no
more Fanshawes. Lady Katherine is dead. The Parliamentary army will have seen to that. I told them to have
their pleasure of her before discarding her. After all, it
is only what you did to me*

There the letter stopped mid-flow. I swayed on my
feet. At first I could not take it in. But then I realised –
Parliament troops were coming. Hadn't Wentworth told
Grice the same? I must warn Lady Katherine. With no

man to protect her, the Roundheads would regard her as spoils of war. There was no time to lose – we would have to leave. Now.

I swiped up the letter and raced upstairs. Lady Katherine read it and understood immediately. 'Lord have mercy,' was all she said. She seemed stunned, unable to move.

'Grice killed Wentworth,' I said. 'His body's in the river.'

She did not ask how I knew, but it spurred her to action. 'Gather my things.' She handed me a leather holdall. 'My pistols are –'

'- in the drawer downstairs. I know,' I said. 'We'll have to get them on the way out.'

'Where is Grice now?'

'In the study. My guess is that in the end he didn't want to share the gold with Wentworth. He did not trust him. He wants to take it all for himself and then get far away from here. His bags are packed. And Parliament troops will be here tonight, I heard Wentworth say so.' I spoke quickly, even though I knew my speech was blurred if I rushed my words. All the time I was shoving things into the bag. 'Quick, let's go whilst Grice is busy. He scares me,' I said.

'Where?'

'The common. Anywhere. Just out of here.' I put my fingers to my lips to gesture to be quiet. I picked up the bag and pulled on her hand. 'Wait! What about your husband's clothes? They could put blame on you.'

'Forget them. They're in the hedge by the packhorse bridge. I was afraid someone would find them in the house.'

'Come then, let's take horse.' We hurried to descend the staircase.

We were about half-way down when Grice's dark figure appeared round the corner. He was dressed for outdoors, his cloak slung back over one shoulder to reveal sword belt and rapier glinting in the half-light.

But it was his pistol that drew my eye.

Lady Katherine stopped dead behind me.

Grice looked at my bags. 'Back upstairs,' Grice said. His voice was like ice.

He advanced on us with the black nose of the barrel pointing at my chest. I was frozen with fear, my legs would not move. Behind Grice the two servants moved in to flank him, hulks of men with blank business-like expressions. Pitman's knife was already drawn, Rigg had a hand on his sword-hilt.

We found our way up the stairs backwards, unwilling to take our eyes away from the gun until Lady Katherine took courage and spoke to Grice. I could not see what she said, but it seemed to provoke Grice more.

'Devil take Simon Fanshawe,' Grice replied. His face glowed an unearthly red in the light streaming through the windows from the setting sun. 'All these years I was loyal to him, looking after his wife's brat, living in the middle of nowhere with second-rate servants. He cheated me - told me you would be married to me one day, but at the last minute he snubbed me. Gave you and your fortune to that cowardly nephew.'

I turned to see Lady Katherine grow wide-eyed at this.

She tried to speak but he took a step nearer with the pistol, and we stumbled another hasty step up the stairs. Lady Katherine gripped my arm as if to give us both strength.

'You never thanked me,' Grice said to her. 'Not once. Not for all my teaching.'

She began to apologize, but he flapped his hand to silence her.

'Too late with your sweet words now. You Fanshawes are all the same. I saved Sir Simon's skin so often, yet never a word of thanks. You find out who your friends really are in battle. He could have cut down the man who severed my foot, he was right there alongside. But he was too lazy a dog to even lift his blade. He saw the roundhead swing his sword but... he just watched it, watched it happen.' The words almost choked him. 'Do you want to know why I hate the Fanshawes?'

We stayed still. We were trapped, and we both knew it. From the corner of my eye I saw my mistress's chest rising and falling.

Grice's mouth trembled as he spoke. 'He left me there. Can you believe it? After all I'd done for him, he watched me topple from my horse and left me to rot in the mud. I was screaming, but did Sir Simon help me? No. Another soldier dragged me away, bound my leg tight, got me to a barber-surgeon before I bled to death.'

Lady Katherine tried to soothe him with words I could not hear.

Grice dragged himself up another step and pushed the nose of the gun up to her chest. The barrel glowed red in the light from the window. 'All those years, a faithful servant. But what does he do? Fires me for being unfit, as if it was my fault, as if *he* had not been there at all. But I'll never forget. Do you know what kept me alive? The thought that I'd get even with him one day. Well, he'll pay now.'

'Please,' I said, 'It's not my mistress's fault, she hates him as much as you do.'

He turned his head slowly to face me. 'So the maid is not as deaf or stupid as she looks.'

'If you hurt her, Sir Simon will hunt you down, you know he will,' I said. 'And the King's men will hang you for treason. Let her go, she's done you no harm.'

'The King's Army is finished. I had a letter from my commander in Scotland, the Scots haven't rallied to the King. His army is a small pack of useless dogs. The King will lose, be beheaded like his father, and Markyate Manor will be forfeit. So I've taken my share now. After

all, it's only what I'm owed. And by the time that coward
Simon Fanshawe returns, if he survives at all, he will
find nothing but dust and debts.'

My mistress tried again to reason with him, 'I'm
sorry for any injustice you feel, but –'

'Shut your mouth. Take her, men.'

The servants rushed up the stairs. A black leather-
clad arm snaked around my neck, choking me. A push
slammed me into the wall in front. I whipped round. We
were backed against the corridor wall, the panelling
pressed into my back next to the mullioned windows. I
still had hold of Lady Katherine's bag in one hand, ready
to run if we got the chance. But we could go nowhere.
Pitman's knife was pressed to my lady's ribs.

The men backed us into Lady Katherine's chamber.
I remembered the wound on Wentworth's back, hoped
for mercy.

'Put her in there,' Grice said to his servants. They
took hold of Lady Katherine roughly by the arms and
pushed her towards the windowless dressing chamber.

'No!' she cried, clawing like a wildcat with her nails
to escape. She knew what they intended. That she'd not
survive when the Parliament troops arrived.

Pitman and Rigg held her back whilst Grice found the
key.

'Let me go in with her,' I said to him, but he shoved
me roughly away.

'Please,' she begged me, 'find Ralph, fetch –' But then her face was gone as Grice turned the key in the lock and I was alone in her chamber with Grice and his men.

Grice turned the pistol on me in one swift movement and pulled the trigger.

But his movement gave me warning and I leapt to the side just as a cloud of smoke issued from the gun. Shock waves from the shot as it hit the wall reverberated in my bones, and a dread certainty. He would kill me.

From the corner of my eye I saw men's fingers reach to grab my arm but I twisted away. Another smatter of wood exploded on the floorboards by the door. I was caught like a rat in a trap. Grice was re-loading and the men backed me towards the fireplace. When I dived I went down like a ferret, down into the priest's hole, the leather bag bumping down with me.

There was no time to think, I scraped down the narrow stairs by feel, shoved my way out into the study.

Over to the desk drawer. I cursed as it stuck. I yanked it, until it suddenly slid out and clattered to the ground. I reached for the pistol case and powder and thrust them into the bag. I scrabbled frantically until I found the leather pouch full of lead shot.

I must get help, get to Ralph.

I bolted from the room just in time. A flash of movement and Rigg's burly frame rounded the corner. I grabbed the door handle and almost fell down the servant's stairs.

Out of the kitchen. Into the stables, my breath coming too fast.

There were only three horses there now, Grice's evil looking beast, Blaze and little Pepper in his stall. The servants' horses must be at the front. I wavered - I needed a horse I could trust. But Pepper would be too slow if they came after me.

I threw on Blaze's bridle, hitched up my skirts, and clambered up some bales of straw to vault astride. I clapped my heels to Blaze's sides and he bolted off. Only by clinging to his mane did I stick there.

Grice and his men ran out and hailed me as I passed the front door, but I could not have stopped even if I'd wanted to. A musket-ball's breath hissed past my cheek but I clung to Blaze's mane. The ground sped by under me with terrifying speed.

The sun had gone and the dusky path ahead of me into the woods was dark. Blaze did not stop. Branches whipped in my face, but I closed my eyes, relied on the grip of my knees. I couldn't go back, and Grice might have sent one of his men after me, so I let the horse carry me through the woods until he suddenly swerved to the left and unseated, I was suddenly in mid-air.

I hit the ground with a thud and sat up coughing, the wind knocked from my lungs. I stumbled to my feet, disorientated but already reaching out for the reins. Blaze was only a few steps away, standing looking forlornly at a fallen tree in our path.

Almost weeping with frustration I stood on the tree to clamber back on, and used my legs to encourage Blaze to jump it, but he refused each time. He was spooked, wild, tossing his head, as if he'd suddenly realised there was an unfamiliar person on his back.

I cursed, hissed 'Go on!' at him. All to no avail. Stupid horse. He'd do it for Lady Katherine. Why not for me?

Either side was a thicket of scrub and brambles. We'd just have to go through there. I kicked him on, but he would not go that way either.

I weighed up the options – turn back and go the long way round, or continue on foot. If I went back I might meet Grice's men. But I didn't want to leave Blaze here in the wood, nor did I want to be without a horse if trouble came my way.

I was wasting time. I wheeled Blaze around and galloped full pelt at the tree. Blaze must have caught my intention for he took off miles away from it and sailed over. I grasped handfuls of his mane to keep myself from falling. The landing jarred my teeth, but we were over.

I slowed to a trot and felt the path soft and squelchy under Blaze's hooves. I looked over my shoulder. All was motionless behind me. No sign of Grice and his men. I hoped my mistress was still alive, that they hadn't already –

But I mustn't think that way. I must get Ralph. He'd know what to do. Help me get my mistress out somehow. But the constable had been adamant he would not release Ralph without bail. It was about a half-mile to the bridge from here I guessed. The bridle path went between two walls, then into more woodland.

Just a little further. A slight sway in the landscape beyond the wall made me pull away into the trees. There were soldiers moving in the far distance across the field. I could not tell whose soldiers, just dark shadows of men moving. But they had to be soldiers, too many men to be anything else. I did not know if there had been any shots, but the men were moving stealthily so I guessed not. Cromwell's men probably. Men with arquebusiers and muskets, I could see their jagged silhouettes. I shuddered. Lady Katherine would not know they were there, closing in.

I kept low over Blaze's neck and wound into the densest part of the wood where there was no path. With a shock I realised I was not afraid, not for myself anyway, my intent was stronger than my fear.

A glint of water alongside me – the river, winding its way to the ford. I looked up, a big straw-coloured moon was just rising over the horizon. *Thank you, thank you*, I thought. Blaze picked his way alongside the water. I guided him where the earth was soft, would make less noise. Finally I saw the packhorse bridge ahead of me, and the ford by it for carriages, the water trickling less than knee-deep.

I paused in the shadow of the trees, watching, like a deer sniffing out danger. A half-formed plan scratched at the back of my mind. I pulled Blaze over into a thicket of trees and hitched him to a branch. I scrambled into the hedge, felt for the bundle Lady Katherine said she had left there. After a few frantic moments I found it, stripped out of my skirts and pulled on the breeches. The belt had holsters for the pistols and I cinched it in to my waist, notched the buckle tightly. It helped me feel more solid. The boots were far too big but they'd make me look more manly. I thrust my skirts into the hedge out of sight. If Lady Katherine could do this, then so could I. Her life depended on it.

I only had to hope that I looked convincing enough to persuade Lady Prescott to hand over the gold.

My fingers shook as I primed the pistols with powder and rammed down the ball by feel. I'd seen my father do it and knew what to do. I had never fired a pistol before in my life. My teeth chattered from cold, or from fright, I could not tell which. I rummaged in the leather bag and brought out the scarf to tie across my face. It smelt faintly of cinnamon and roses and the scent brought tears to my eyes and almost made me lose my courage.

I wondered briefly if I was mad. I could just gallop on. But where would I go? My mother was at the smith's. Ralph was in gaol. And Lady Katherine was at this very minute awaiting a fate worse than I could imagine.

I jammed the hat down over my forehead. The moon lit up the path, but there was no sign of any carriage. I lifted one of the pistols from my belt, felt its solid weight in my right hand. The reins were damp and greasy in my other, and I felt the slight shake of Blaze's head.

A moment where I realised what I had become, what I had to do. It seemed unreal, that I was here. I suddenly felt alone, insubstantial, like a shadow carved out of the air. I turned my head, scanning the trees and the road for movement. Nothing. It was as if the world held its breath.

CHAPTER TWENTY-ONE

Pistol and Shot

The coach and pair appeared from nowhere – a blur of hooves and wheels. It slowed to ford the water and I saw the gold of the monogram on the side as it rocked and trembled down the bank. But as it entered the water the wheels slewed to a stop, throwing up water and stones.

I kicked Blaze on, onto the bridge and round to stand in their path.

They must see me, they must.

For a moment the elderly coachman gathered his reins and I thought he might drive his pair over me, but I raised the pistol and yelled in the deepest voice I could, 'Stop! Stand down!'

He slid from his perch and scuttled into the water. I saw him take cover behind the coach.

I pulled Blaze round and cantered down the bank to approach the side window. The occupants of the coach were already half-out. Lady Prescott almost fell out into the water in her haste to get away. But a thick-set man in leather armour was giving her cover. He let loose a shot with his snub-nosed musket and I saw the flare of his tinder, the jerk as he recoiled. Smoke blasted out of the muzzle. Blaze shied as the shot hit a tree, but I clung on, held Blaze under control.

The acrid smell of powder and shot made me cough, but I held my nerve, kept the gun pointing at Lady Prescott.

'Please,' she cried, 'have mercy!'

I could not pull the trigger. My moment's hesitation was all she needed, she scrambled away under the bridge for cover, dragging her sodden skirts behind her.

The guard was re-loading. I knew there was not much time. I flung myself off Blaze and down to the ground and waded to the coach. The coachman had uncoupled one of the horses and, with surprising agility, he vaulted on and I watched his broad back gallop away down the path. Two more steps and I was at the coach door.

Another shot blasted a hole in the door right next to my hand, and the force of it made the open door swing. I kept the gun pointing back, as I felt desperately over the floor and seats with my other hand, but I could find nothing.

No box, no pouch, no gold.

I was confused, but then saw Lady Prescott peering at me from the bridge. Lady Prescott's man, seeing my intent, sploshed through the shallows towards her, clumsily trying to re-load his gun as he went, but he was not quick enough – I got to Lady Prescott first.

I pressed my pistol to her temple. 'Where's the gold?' 'There is no gold,' she screamed.

'Deliver me the gold,' I repeated, unwilling to believe it.

'It was a trick, a ruse,' she shouted. I wanted to be sure I'd understood right.

I pressed the muzzle harder into her soft skin. 'Tell me.'

About a man's length away her guard stood still, his musket pointing to the sky, hands up. He was asking me not to fire.

'Tell me,' I repeated.

'We suspect Grice is a spy,' she whimpered, 'so we set a trap to catch him. But you'll get your come-uppance - the King's Army should be here by now to catch him.'

I had an urge to pull the trigger, but stopped myself in time. What was I turning into? Anyway, it would serve no use. I floundered away, the disappointment threatening to overwhelm me. No gold. So it was all for nothing. Disaster.

I let out a ragged breath. The noise of fire would bring every soldier for miles around, I knew. According to Lady Prescott, Royalist troops were already on their way here, and Parliament troops to the Manor not two miles away. Soon I would be sitting in a bloody battle-field.

I had failed. I could not get Ralph out, and Lady Katherine would die.

My emotion made me careless, and as I moved away from Lady Prescott the manservant lunged towards me. His grip on my pistol arm bit through my sleeve. It brought me to my senses. Frustration made me blind with rage. I twisted and cursed, but he pinioned my pistol behind my back. I kicked out at his ankle and brought my other knee up hard against his groin. He almost let go, staggered on his feet.

A wild blur of black emerged from the trees. Another figure on horseback galloping along the bank. He shouted something from the bridge and waved a long rifle. I thought he might run us down, the horse forged through the shallows towards us.

It was all over. If it was one of the King's Men, others would follow close behind.

The guard let go, put his hands up. I did the same. My thoughts raced. What would the King's soldiers do to me when they found out I'd threatened Lady Prescott?

The man on the bank was familiar. The set of his shoulders, the tilt of his head. Surely it couldn't be?

But I would recognise my brother anywhere.

'Ralph!' I yelled.

He glanced briefly over his shoulder, looking for the source of the voice. It was enough time for the man by my side to raise his musket to his shoulder. At the same time Ralph took aim. Undistracted by the noise of firing I had a clear view of how the recoil from the guard's musket jerked it off target whereas Ralph's aim was sharp and true.

The guard staggered, fell backwards into the water. It parted to receive him then splashed back over him. He floundered only a moment, bubbles escaping from his mouth and nose, then was still. The moon had come out again from behind the clouds and I was transfixed by the body next to me, oozing ink-like blood into the water.

Lady Prescott cowered further under the bridge. Ralph kept one of his weapons pointed at me, as he gestured for her to come out onto the bridge. Then I realised. He still did not know who I was.

'For mercy's sake! Ralph!' I cried, 'It's me, Abi! Don't shoot!'

His hand wavered, dropped down. He dismounted in one fluid movement and was at my side in an instant, his pistol before him, his face full of suspicion. I tore away my scarf with my free hand.

His eyes widened. He grabbed hold of the scarf and tossed it into the river. 'What do you think you're doing? You stupid girl? You could get yourself killed! Of all the tomfool –'

'She's getting away!' I pointed to Lady Prescott who had gathered up her skirts and was heading into the trees. 'Stop, or I'll fire,' I yelled.

Lady Prescott's eyes swivelled towards me as I went up the bank.

'Don't shoot,' she begged, flinging up her hands.

'Then stay still,' I said. The pistol felt cold and weighty against my palm, and I pointed it at her in what I hoped was a threatening manner.

A glance to Ralph showed his amazed expression, but I didn't dare move my gun from Lady Prescott.

'Wait there,' Ralph said.

'No,' I called, but he had already waded through the ford and was looking inside the coach. A few moments later and he was back at my side.

'Are we too late?' he asked, automatically signing with his free hand.

'No. It's empty,' I said. 'But there's no time for that. Kate's in danger, we must go back to the Manor, get past Grice somehow. He has sent Parliament men there. They'll be there at first light and they're after Royalist blood. They'll kill her if we can't get her out.'

'What about her?' Ralph said, indicating Lady Prescott.

'Just leave her,' I said. 'Her friends are on the way, let them look to her.'

I lowered my gun and Lady Prescott ran off into the woods in a blur of skirt and petticoat.

'Listen,' Ralph said.

I could hear nothing, but I felt a slight tremor through the soles of my boots.

'Horses,' I whispered. 'It could be the King's men, Lady Prescott's expecting them.'

We pulled off the main track and into the trees.

The horsemen drew up, a little way off, and seeing the coach with only one horse in the traces and its door hanging open, began to arm themselves. I froze – even from here I could see it was Grice and his serving men. I crept away from Blaze, hid myself behind a thicket of hawthorn.

Ralph had pulled his horse back into the shadows. Grice and Rigg rode ahead first. They passed close to me on the track, pistols at the ready. The third man, Pitman, followed behind on a hired mare, his eyes scanning left and right.

To my horror, Blaze lowered his head and moved forward onto the path. Stupid horse. Now they'd know we were here.

Pitman shouted something to the other men and they halted. There was a discussion which I could not hear, but they dismounted and Grice continued limping towards the ford and the coach, whilst his two servants moved pincer-like into the woods. I crouched lower. They were looking for me.

I saw a flash as Pitman spotted Ralph behind the tree and let loose a shot. But my brother was quicker - a blast of air and a musket-ball from my brother toppled Pitman. Riggs dived for cover. Grice splashed into the stream and crouched down behind the coach. From there he took aim at Ralph, who was masked by a big oak.

Riggs hadn't seen me and began to work his way through the thicket to creep up on Ralph. Grice tried another shot but it glanced off the tree. I saw Ralph's white stock disappear as he whipped behind the trunk into cover.

Riggs was closer to Ralph now, with a prowling intent look. He stopped, closed one eye, raised his pistol before him with both hands, slowly took aim at Ralph's head.

A red mist seemed to blur my eyes. Wildly, I lifted my pistol pointed it at Rigg and fired. The recoil took it off target, but my other pistol was ready. I fired again. This time Rigg fell. But I kept pressing the triggers even though the fire was dead and my palms smarted from the kick of the gun.

Rigg did not get up. I was taken by surprise that it was so quick. I'd shot a man.

Grice blundered out from behind the coach, head down, grabbing for branches to support himself as he had no stick. He was making for his horse. Ralph sprinted after him and tussled him to the ground. He pressed his musket to Grice's chest.

Grice whimpered and writhed.

Ralph turned to me, 'Your belt,' he said.

'This?' I pulled it from round my waist. He took off his own.

'Get up,' he said to Grice.

'I can't,' he whined, 'My leg.'

'Then crawl.'

Without his servants muscle-power Grice had become lily-livered. We secured him to the coach wheel. I tied his arms to the spokes, while Ralph kept the gun to his chest. I tore off his wooden foot and threw the disgusting thing as far as I could downstream where it floated away. Grice lay half-propped up, only his head and chest out of the water. 'I beg you, don't leave me here,' he said.

'The key,' I said, 'to the dressing room.'

'In my pouch,' he said.

I unclipped his pouch and shook out the coins until I found the key. 'Come on,' I dragged on Ralph's sleeve. For I remembered the men I had seen in the fields, moving south.

Ralph withdrew the gun from Grice's chest. 'If Lady Katherine has come to any harm, I'll come back and shoot you.'

CHAPTER TWENTY-TWO

A Son's Duty

Ralph galloped ahead and I followed. My chest hurt, as if my heart had already been bruised too much. The nights were short at this time of the year and the sky was already lightening above us. When we reached the grounds of Markyate Manor we could see the shapes of pikes moving forwards on the other side of the hedge, and a great rabble of a regiment moving down the long drive.

Just the sight of all those men made my stomach turn to water. When we got around the side of the house Ralph reined in his horse.

'Where is she?' he said.

I signed, 'Upstairs.'

'You'll have to show me,' he said. He slid down and followed me.

We left the horses where they stood and raced across the cobbled yard in a few strides. The kitchen door was still swinging ajar. It seemed years since I had left.

Even as we opened the door from the servant's stairs on to the landing, Ralph stopped, his head cocked, listening. His hand tensed around his sword.

'They've got in already,' he whispered. I went to the front window to look out. What was left of the formation was led by two cavalry officers with a Parliament standard, and a few more brought up the rear with a rolling cannon. The lawns were littered with covered wagons – the baggage train that went everywhere with the troops, carrying powder for the cannon and grain for the horses. Surrounding the wagons was a motley bunch of camp followers – women and old men with the tools of their trade – the barber-surgeon, the farrier, the gunsmith.

But it was not these that made my blood freeze in my veins. Everywhere streamed soldiers, running towards the house.

'God in heaven,' I said.

I threw open the door to the servants stairs with Ralph close behind, but we were too late. Three blood-stained soldiers were already on the way down. One of them rushed by us, dragging the quilt from the bed and a ticking pillow. He slit it with his knife shaking the feathers out on the floor in a cloud of brown and white.

Ralph was so shocked he could only stare. The man took up a candlestick from the side table and stuffed it into the pillowcase. They forced us to the side as they barged by, leaving us coughing in a sea of feathers. We hurried up towards the bedchambers.

The doors were splintered from their hinges. On the first floor landing a group of men already had Lady Katherine by the arms. Her forehead was bleeding and her eyes wide with terror. A bearded infantryman was trying to lift her skirts, and the others were laughing, mouths jeering insults. A strong smell of drink and sweat accompanied them.

'A little fun, gentlemen?' said the bearded man to me. Of course, I was still dressed like a boy. Ralph was suddenly still. It was only then that I realised I knew him.

It was Father.

Ralph pointed his musket at him. 'Leave her be.'

'Ralph? Father let go of my mistress's skirts and made to embrace him, but Ralph kept the musket levelled at him.

'Keep away. Don't dare touch me! I'm ashamed of you. Is this what you do? Terrify young women, rob and plunder, even in your own village?'

'Come on now, Ralph, it was only a bit of –'

''Fun' were you going to say? Would you like soldiers to do the same to our Abigail? Is this fun?' He shoved his musket into Father's throat.

'Ralph!' I cried, 'For pity's sake!' I dare not move, I thought he might fire. Father looked blearily into my face, and I saw the recognition dawn. 'Abigail?' His lips said my name, but then his eyes slid away. He could not look me in the face.

Some of the other men laughed, sniggered behind their hands. Lady Katherine was ashen, her head pulled backwards by the soldier who still had hold of her hair.

'Leave go,' Ralph said to him, 'or I fire.'

Father looked down at the pistol and gave a nervous laugh, 'You wouldn't –'

'She's not the enemy, Father!' I said. 'It's my friend Kate, one of my mistress's serving maids.'

'Serving maid, lady, what's the difference? They're all tarred with the Fanshawe brush.' The soldier gave a vicious tug on Lady Katherine's hair.

Ralph's face was white with anger, 'She's my sweetheart,' he said, 'I love her.'

Father tried to save face by laughing and moving away but Ralph would not give up, kept his gun to Father's throat. 'Tell them to leave her alone,' he said, 'or I'm warning you I won't be responsible for what I do.'

A moment where father and son looked at each other like strangers, both unwilling to give in. I held my breath, not daring to move. *Please, for mercy's sake, Ralph, don't shoot*, I prayed.

A moment more, then Father sagged away from the gun. 'Let her go,' he said. The soldier clung on. 'It's an order,' he snapped.

Ralph moved over and took hold of Lady Katherine by the arm. Her face was wet with tears of terror.

I took hold of her other hand and wrung it tight.

'We're leaving now,' Ralph said, 'and I don't expect to be stopped. My father will remind you that you are civilised men, not beasts. Isn't that right?'

My father had lost all his bravado. He looked to be a sad, confused little man now. I wondered that anyone would take orders from him. Just as I was thinking this, a big-chested man entered the room, and my father straightened up, saluted him.

The other man seemed calm. He had a lazy air of authority and the ragged bunch of men stood to attention. 'What's going on? Who are these women?'

'Servants, Colonel Greene,' said my father. 'My son is escorting them to the village.'

'And what's happened to discipline?'

'The men are just a little lively,' my father said, not meeting his eyes. 'Soldiers will be soldiers.'

The Colonel turned his attention to Ralph. 'You are Chaplin's son?'

Ralph nodded.

'The one who has taken Cromwell's shilling to join us?'

'To my shame, yes.' He gave the Colonel a look of flint. Then he bowed, and pushing Lady Katherine ahead of him strode out of the door. I followed, without looking back. Little did I know then, that it would be the last time I would ever see my father.

As we walked through the house we saw soldiers tearing it apart for anything of value. My legs felt as though they did not belong to me. We passed another soldier hauling the tapestry drapes from the window. He gave a final pull until the whole rail came down. He pushed past us with his prize, before Colonel Greene yelled at him from the top of the stairs, and he was forced to drop it sheepishly to the ground.

Ralph did not let go of Kate, his arm was around her waist, and I held her on the other side. As we passed through the yard, we walked by small knots of soldiers hunched in groups, dividing up the spoils of the house, arguing and cursing over tankards and candlesticks. Inside the manor, blurred shapes still ran past the windows. But we did not stop. Instinctively I moved closer to Lady Katherine as the men bawled at each other and snatched the spoils from each other's grip.

When Lady Katherine turned to speak to me I saw she could not manage the words. She held herself upright as if afraid to let go, closed her mouth.

None of us spoke. We just kept on walking. We walked on until we came to the edge of the common, where Ralph stopped. The sky was pale and vast above us.

'The birds are singing,' he whispered.

'Just like any other day,' I said.

Ralph held out his arms and Lady Katherine fell into them as if she had waited for it all her life. He crushed her to his chest. I saw his lips murmur, 'Safe now,' over and over before I turned away embarrassed as he kissed her hair.

A long time later she came to touch me on the shoulder. 'You saved me from... ' she could not say the words. When I held out my arms, her embrace was tight, like a sister.

After she let me go, I said to Ralph, 'Where shall we go? We can't go back to the Manor.'

'Jacob will give us rest and a place to stay. He's sweet on you, Abi. It was to please you that he persuaded his father to let me go. But on condition I signed up for the New Model Army. Jacob's father thought it would help keep me out of trouble.'

That was a jest all right. But I couldn't believe that, about Jacob. Ralph must only be saying it. 'But what about Lady Katherine?' I asked, 'Is there room for her too?'

'Don't call me that, please,' she said. 'Plain Kate will do.'

'She stays with me,' Ralph said. 'But it's only one night. The regiment will be moving on tomorrow to go to Worcester, and maybe it will be safe then for you both to return to the Manor.'

'I'm not sure I want to go back. It does not feel like I belong there any more. It's all spoilt. The troops have destroyed what five generations have made. My mother would have wept to see it.'

'Then it's a mercy she can't.' Ralph said, taking hold of her hand and interlacing his fingers with hers.

She smiled shyly, but then the smile was replaced by a worried frown.

'What is it?' Ralph asked her.

'I was thinking about Grice.'

'He won't come back,' Ralph said. We met him on the road – left him where his so-called Royalist friends could find him. They know he's a spy, and I don't suppose they'll show him much forgiveness.'

Lady Katherine's face was still troubled. She let go of Ralph's hand and stepped away, 'But if word gets to my stepfather and my husband, they will –'

'Let's not talk of them,' Ralph said firmly, drawing her back into his arms. 'The sun is coming up and it's going to be a beautiful day. Tomorrow will take care of itself, I dare say.'

CHAPTER TWENTY-THREE

Farewell

We spent the next day at Jacob's cottage. Kate and I took Jacob's bedchamber and he and Ralph slept downstairs in the kitchen where they could be ready with swords if any more trouble should come. Kate said they talked a long time, she could hear their voices murmuring below. I slept like I had not slept for months, with Kate next to me to hear for me, and knowing we were safe.

We rose again late in the afternoon, ready to eat and make plans. Jacob made us tell him the tale of the night's events as we feasted on bread and barley soup. I was embarrassed, for I had only my boy's clothes, and it made me aware of the shape of my legs, on display for all to see, and not hidden under skirts as they should be. I caught Jacob looking, so I sat down hurriedly and pushed my legs underneath the table.

Kate was pale and tired-looking, but composed.

'I'm sorry, Kate, I will have to go with the regiment,' Ralph said.

'Do you have to?' I asked.

'I took Cromwell's shilling as part of the bail, and failure to report counts as desertion. You know what the penalty is for that.'

The noose. 'Give it back then,' I said.

'Once in your hand it is a pledge. It should only be a short campaign though, and our troops will win. When I was talking with… when I enlisted they told me that the Scots have failed the King, and that it will be over in a day. Never fear, you won't be rid of me for long.'

I saw how he was careful not to mention my father as he spoke. My heart blessed him.

'When is the muster?'

'Dawn tomorrow in the town square.'

'What will you do, Kate?' I asked.

She traced a fingertip on the table, did not look up. 'Last night I dreamt of my mother. She was walking in the rose garden at the front of the house. The sun was on the grass and the windows sparkled with light. I knew she wanted me to bring the Manor back to life. A resurrection, if you like. And then there are the tenants, like your mother. I will give them their cottages back, if after all that's happened, I can sort out the mess and they want to come.'

Ralph had turned away, hurt.

She looked towards him and spoke up, 'I'll never forget the Diggers, but I know I'm not free to make a Digger's life. My stepfather would kill anyone who came between me and Thomas's affections. If he was to hear about Ralph - if anyone were to breathe a single word – then he would show no mercy. I'm going back to Markyate Manor not because I don't care, but because I care too much.'

Ralph turned at this, and such a look of longing hung there that it made me blush.

The evening was spent in quiet conversation. Jacob had borrowed some clothes for us from the alms box at his father's house, so that when the cock crowed the next morning both Kate and I had dressed by the candlelight in brown homespun and faded linen caps.

When it got light, a noise from outside drew Kate to the window. It was the baggage train setting off for the muster in the square. We watched the oxen and carts trundle by with their deadly loads of powder kegs and pikes. We were fascinated but sobered to watch it pass, with so many tented wagons like a great city on the move. We went downstairs to tell Ralph and Jacob, but they were already dressed and by the window.

'The infantry won't be far behind them,' Jacob said, 'Are you ready?'

'As ready as I will ever be,' Ralph said.

'Then best say your farewells whilst there's time.'

Kate waited for him to embrace her, but he was suddenly awkward. He went to the door and opened it, stood on the threshold. Jacob and I exchanged glances. Neither of us would want to be in his shoes, preparing to put down his life for Parliament.

Kate approached him from behind, wound her arms around his waist, until he turned, looked her gravely in the face. He seemed to see what he wanted, and smiling, lifted her off her feet, kissed her on the lips. When he put her down his eyes were full of unshed tears and he strode away in sudden haste, without even a word.

'Keep safe!' Kate cried after him.

We ran out into the street to watch his back as he went. We shouted, 'Farewell! God Speed!' waving our kerchiefs like frantic fools.

Kate was a long time coming in. Jacob and I had swept the hearth, washed the churns and collected the eggs by the time she came.

'He'll be alright,' I said, to cheer her.

I tried not to think about the musketeers that had marched down the road after him. And the fact that the King would have armed men just like them.

Kate picked up an egg from the bowl, cupped it gently in her hand before placing it back. 'I know I have no right to ask, Abi, but would you come back to the Manor with me? I don't think I can manage without my friend.'

'Like a companion you mean?'

'If you'll come. It will be hard, waiting for news. And there will always be work for you where I am – that is, if you want it.' She looked down, as if fearing I might say no.

'You mean you'll be needing someone to scrub now the troops have gone,' I said laughing.

'No, no – I meant –'

'I know,' I said, softly, putting my hand on her arm. 'I was jesting. Of course I'll come. I would not let you go back there alone.'

So it was settled. Jacob's father had heard of the disturbance and had gone over to the Manor, but had found it deserted. Nevertheless, we waited until late in the afternoon to go back. We did not want to meet any troops on the way, and we needed to make sure they had gone from the Manor. Jacob could not come with us as he'd promised to meet his father that afternoon. But he gave us a pack pony carrying provisions and other essential things he thought we might need.

'I wish I could come with you,' Jacob said.

'We'll be careful,' Kate said.

'I'll ride over this evening, if it's alright. And I was wondering – when you have a day off Abigail, whether we might walk out together.'

'I'd love to,' I said before wondering if I'd heard him right and before he could change his mind. He gave an almighty grin and I felt like my heart might boil over.

'Just tell us which day, and she'll be there,' Kate said.

Jacob Mallinson had asked me out! I smiled then as if my cheeks might crack.

Kate and I walked to the Manor in the late afternoon heat, arm in arm. The building rose from the ground just the way it had, months before. Except that now it was familiar, I knew every inch of that house. I was the one who'd polished it and swept it and made it shine. And now it felt as though it could be my home.

We stopped about an acre away. We were both wondering what lay within, whether we could bear to see the shell of it. Kate set off towards the front door, then at the last moment turned to go in at the back. In we went, through the deserted kitchen, up the servant stairs and into the empty hall.

We stood in the silence. Sunlight streamed in over the dust formed by hundreds of tramping feet.

'We'll soon bring it back to how it was,' I said.

'No,' Kate said, 'Not how it was. A new beginning, like the Diggers said. There'll be no more orders from me, we'll work together.'

My gaze took in the overturned chairs, the bare windows and the doors gouged with the marks of bayonets. Yet somehow it didn't seem daunting.

I could not wait to get started. 'Come on then, Kate,' I said, 'best roll up your sleeves.'

Roundheads and Cavaliers

In the middle of the seventeenth century, England went to war – not with another country, but with itself. This was a war which spread to Scotland, Wales and Ireland and to all levels of society. The dispute was one in which both men and women were prepared to take sides on matters of principle, and fight for their beliefs to the death.

In simple terms, the War was one between the King and his followers – the King's Army, and Parliament on the other – The New Model Army, led by Cromwell. Sometimes these groups are known as Cavaliers and Roundheads. 'Cavalier' from the Spanish, *caballero*, originally meant a mounted soldier, but came to be used as an insult to denote someone who would put themselves above their station. 'Roundhead' was a term used to describe the short-haired apprentices who first came out in favour of Parliament.

The fighting was over matters of political policy, and on how Britain should be governed. The differences between the two factions were complicated by their differing religious views; the Anglicanism of the King versus the Puritanism of Cromwell's men. The War began when the port of Hull refused to open its gates to the King, and in 1642 the King proclaimed war on his rebellious subjects.

The English Civil War killed about two hundred thousand people, almost four percent of the population, and brought disease and famine in its wake. It divided families and stripped the land of food and wealth, as troops rampaged the countryside foraging and plundering whatever they could find.

Towns were flattened, and communities dispersed. For example, records show that Parliamentary troops blew up more than two hundred houses at Leicester just to provide a clear line of fire, whilst four hundred more were destroyed at Worcester and another two hundred at Faringdon.

There were nearly ten years of fighting and unrest. Some children barely knew their fathers as they had been away in the wars for most of that time. In effect there were three main periods of fighting, and this book is set between the last two bouts, when the King is about to make his last stand against Cromwell's increasingly efficient New Model Army.

The seventeenth century saw a King executed, followed by the establishment of what could be viewed as a military dictatorship under Cromwell. It was also a time that transformed society, and gave birth to new ideas about political and religious liberty, as demonstrated by the Diggers and sundry other sects with alternative or utopian ideals.

The Diggers

The Diggers were the first group of people to try and live in what we would nowadays call a 'commune.' Led by Gerrard Winstanley, the movement began in Cobham, Surrey in 1649, but rapidly spread to other parishes in the southern area of England.

The Diggers advocated equality for all, even equality between men and women, which was viewed as a radical idea in the seventeenth century. Their ideas also included the sharing of all goods and property, the replacement of money with bartering, and the ability to worship freely in whatever way one chose.

The name 'The Diggers' came from Winstanley's belief that the earth was made to be 'a common treasury for all', and that all should be able to dig it, and provide themselves with what was necessary for human survival – food, warmth and shelter. The Diggers made several unsuccessful attempts to build houses in different locations, but were suppressed by the land-owning classes and dispersed by force, and the communities wiped out. Although the Diggers were a short-lived movement, their ideas had a far-reaching effect, sowing the seeds of communal living and self-sufficiency for future generations.

The Real Lady Katherine Fanshawe

Lady Katherine Fanshawe really did exist. Katherine was born on 4th May 1634 into a wealthy family, the Ferrers. Tragically, her father, Knighton Ferrers, died two weeks before she was born, and her grandfather shortly after, leaving her the sole heir to a fortune.

A few years later her mother was married again, to the spendthrift and gambler Sir Simon Fanshawe. Unfortunately, Katherine's mother died when she was only eight, leaving her at the mercy of the Fanshawe family. Sir Simon supported the Royalist cause and the King needed money to fund his army. Sir Simon conceived of a plan to marry off his nephew, Thomas Fanshawe, to the rich heiress, thus gaining control over Katherine's wealth and land.

This is where my book begins! But the stories about Lady Katherine that I found really fascinating were the reports of her exploits as a notorious highwaywoman. The legend has been handed down through the generations, and the story of her night-time raids has been made into a film entitled, 'The Wicked Lady.'

Whilst researching this book I took into account both the real history and the legend. I also discovered that Lady Ann Fanshawe, who features in my story, wrote a diary, and I used this as part of my research. There are no historical records about Ralph Chaplin, although his name always appears in the stories. I have taken the liberty of giving him a fictional family, including a sister called Abigail. Lady Katherine Fanshawe (Kate), Ralph and Abigail will also appear in the next book of the series, 'Ghost on the Highway,' which will be Ralph's part of the legend, and in 'Lady of the Highway', which will be the final part of Katherine's story.

The Character of Abigail

I chose to have a deaf girl as my main character because there was a remarkable flowering of education and knowledge in the seventeenth century about how to help non-hearing children communicate. The early members of the Royal Society of London had the idea of creating a universal language, and developed several different strands of research including the teaching of phonetics and the beginnings of sign language. When I came across this in my research, it sparked my interest, and gave me the idea for Abigail. Of course there are many differing degrees of deafness and every person is different and unique. What works for some, will be unworkable for others. For the particular character of Abigail I am grateful to the excellent autobiography 'What's that Pig Outdoors — A Memoir of Deafness' by Henry Kisor, who lost his hearing at the age of three to meningitis.

More on the education of deaf children in the 17th Century can be found in these resources:

Alexander Popham's Notebook
(Britsh Deaf History Society - facsimile of the 17th century notebook)
Video - History of Deaf Education: www.bslzone.co.uk
British Deaf Association www.bda.org.uk

From Deborah

I hope you have enjoyed my notes. More information about my research for this book and my writing life can be found on my website www.deborahswift.com, or chat to me on Twitter @swiftstory

CPSIA information can be obtained at www.ICGtesting.com
Printed in the USA
LVOW07s1618060715

445136LV00006B/609/P